The start of something...

"I can tell you how you're luckier than Austin Chadwick."

"This ought to be good."

She took another couple of steps toward me, close enough now that I could smell her shampoo, a soapy peach scent that I got to know very well later. She counted on her fingers. They were long and white, with perfectly curved nails. I wanted to touch them, but I didn't. "One, you're smarter than Austin. Two, you're probably *not* an alcoholic. Three, you're better looking than he is. Four, you've got the balls to wade out into the Willis River with me."

"That's some list."

She laughed low in her throat and took one more step, and now I could feel the heat coming off her skin. "You still think Austin has it better than you? You'd rather be sprawled out on the floor of the country club men's room than here with me?"

"Not especially."

That's when she kissed me.

OTHER BOOKS YOU MAY ENJOY

the
secret
year

the secret year

JENNIFER R. HUBBARD

speak

An Imprint of Penguin Group (USA) Inc.

SPEAK
Published by the Penguin Group
Penguin Group (USA) Inc., 345 Hudson Street, New York, New York 10014, U.S.A.
Penguin Group (Canada), 90 Eglinton Avenue East, Suite 700,
Toronto, Ontario, Canada M4P 2Y3 (a division of Pearson Penguin Canada Inc.)
Penguin Books Ltd, 80 Strand, London WC2R 0RL, England
Penguin Ireland, 25 St Stephen's Green, Dublin 2, Ireland (a division of Penguin Books Ltd)
Penguin Group (Australia), 250 Camberwell Road, Camberwell, Victoria 3124, Australia
(a division of Pearson Australia Group Pty Ltd)
Penguin Books India Pvt Ltd, 11 Community Centre,
Panchsheel Park, New Delhi - 110 017, India
Penguin Group (NZ), 67 Apollo Drive, Rosedale, North Shore 0632, New Zealand
(a division of Pearson New Zealand Ltd)
Penguin Books (South Africa) (Pty) Ltd, 24 Sturdee Avenue,
Rosebank, Johannesburg 2196, South Africa

Registered Offices: Penguin Books Ltd, 80 Strand, London WC2R 0RL, England

First published in the United States of America by Viking,
a member of Penguin Group (USA) Inc., 2010

Published by Speak, an imprint of Penguin Group (USA) Inc., 2011

3 5 7 9 10 8 6 4 2

THE LIBRARY OF CONGRESS HAS CATALOGED THE VIKING EDITION AS FOLLOWS:
Hubbard, Jennifer R.
The secret year / by Jennifer Hubbard.
p. cm.
Summary: Reading the journal of the high-society girl he was secretly involved with for a
year helps high school senior Colt cope with her death and come closer to understanding
why she needed him while continuing to be the girlfriend of a wealthy classmate.
ISBN: 978-0-670-01153-7 (hc)
[1. Dating (Social customs)—Fiction. 2. Social classes—Fiction. 3. Secrets—Fiction.
4. Death—Fiction. 5. High schools—Fiction. 6. Schools—Fiction. 7. Diaries—Fiction.]
I. Title
PZ7.H8582Sec 2010
[Fic]—dc22
2009015179
Speak ISBN 978-0-14-241779-9

Printed in the United States of America

Set in Minion
Book design by Sam Kim

the
secret
year

chapter 1

Julia was killed on Labor Day on her way home from a party. I didn't get to see her that night. I used to meet her on Friday nights, but I was never invited to the parties that she was invited to. We'd meet on the banks of the river, clutch at each other in the backseat of her car, steam up her windows and write messages and jokes to each other in the fog on the glass, and argue about whether to turn on the A/C. Sometimes we swam in the river late at night when the water was black and no one could see us. We did all that for a year, and nobody else knew.

There were a couple of reasons we never told anybody about us. For one thing, she lived up on Black Mountain Road, in a house that was five times as big as mine. With servants. And a computerized alarm system that looked like it should've been running the space program instead of protecting one house. At my place, we just had a sign my father tacked up in our yard that said TRESPASSERS WILL BE SHOT.

We didn't have anything worth stealing anyway. I lived on the flats off Higgins Farm Road, where there were no farms left anymore, in a house with my father's junked cars all over the yard. Every couple of years the township gave my dad a ticket and tried to get him to clear out our property, but he basically told them to go to hell. When I was little, I liked to play in those cars. I used to imagine I could help get them running again. But by the time I was fifteen, I realized those wrecks were never going to move again unless they were dragging behind a tow truck.

Anyway, that was the biggest difference between Julia and me: Black Mountain versus the flats. Not that we were Romeo and Juliet or anything. Nobody was trying to keep us apart. My family wouldn't have cared if I'd gone out with her. Julia's family probably would've hated me, but they wouldn't have locked her in her room. It was what her friends would've thought that bothered her, I think. Besides, she already had a boyfriend: Austin Chadwick. His name always sounded fake to me, like the kind an actor would give himself. She was with him that last night.

Austin lived on Black Mountain, too, with his expensive car and his expensive clothes. I have to admit, though, the cars and clothes didn't bother me as much as the way he strutted around like he was *entitled* to what he had, instead of realizing he was born into it, dumb-ass lucky.

Was I jealous that he could go anywhere he wanted with Julia, that they ate at the same lunch table and made out in front of the drinking fountain? Hell, no. I didn't want to be her boyfriend. Things were better the way they were. She used to drive down to the bridge near my house in her little black car, and I'd meet her there. I guess I would've liked to *talk* to her at school, though. Not to have to pretend we didn't know each other. When she passed me in the halls, her eyes would glide over me like I was part of the walls. That turned me cold. I liked to break that glide, to catch and hold her eyes.

Usually nobody else was looking, but once her friend Pam noticed. She nudged Julia, leaned in, and whispered in her ear. Julia laughed and flipped her hair back as if to say, "Who, that guy? I was just staring into space, and he happened to be in the way."

I heard about the accident a few hours after it happened. It was Labor Day—night, actually. The house was too quiet because my brother, Tom, had just gone off to his first year of college. I wasn't used to the stillness yet. Before, I had always heard his stereo, or his hammering away at weird projects, like the twelve-foot abstract wooden "sculpture" he built in the backyard.

I was on my bed, listening to the rain and trying to decide whether to go into the kitchen for another bowl of cornflakes (and hear my mother say for the ten millionth time, "Colten, do you have a tapeworm?") or keep lying there and fall asleep, which would mean waking up starving around two in the morning.

The phone rang then. I rolled over to grab it. "Colt?" my friend Sydney said. I knew she recognized my voice, but she always sounded tentative, as if she might've dialed the wrong number.

"Hi, Syd."

"Did you hear about the accident?"

"What accident?"

"Up on Black Mountain Road. Julia Vernon got killed, and Pam Henderson's in the hospital."

I sat up. "Who told you that?"

"Kirby. The Hendersons called her to babysit Pam's brother when they went to the hospital."

I got out of bed and started to walk up and down the space between my bed and desk. "Are you sure?"

"All I know is what Kirby said. She seemed pretty sure."

I didn't say anything. I kept pacing.

"I bet they were drunk. There was a big party at Adam Hancock's all day—his parents are in Greece."

"Were they in Austin's car? Was he with them?"

"No, it was just the two of them, in Pam's car."

Well, they sure as hell couldn't have been in Julia's. I knew her car was in the shop, and I also knew why, but I couldn't tell Syd any of that.

"What else did you hear?" I asked.

"Not much. But Kirby thinks Pam is going to be okay."

Syd wasn't part of the Black Mountain crowd any more than I was. After all, she lived on the flats, and she hung around with people like me. But she kept tabs on the Black Mountain kids as if she were a reporter for a celebrity gossip show. Syd got her information from friends like Kirby Matthews, who lived at the base of Black Mountain and didn't fully belong to either the mountain or the flats crowd. Most of the time, when Syd told me the latest from the grapevine, I couldn't care less. That night I did care. That night I wanted to know everything.

I got off the phone with Syd as soon as I realized she didn't know any more than she'd said already. I called Julia's cell phone. I had never done that unless I was sure she wanted me to and sure she'd be alone. Now I called anyway. I wanted her to tell me the gossip was wrong, that she was fine. I would've even been happy to have her pissed at me for calling.

Nobody answered. I got her usual message. "Hi there, it's Julia, and my phone's off because I'm the only person in the world who doesn't want the rest of civilization listening to my calls. Leave a message, the juicier the better, extra points for creativity, and I'll listen to it when I'm alone." I hung up before the beep and sat on my bed, trying to figure out what to do next.

I couldn't help thinking of the last time we'd seen each other, the fight we'd had. We'd made up afterward, but it was one of those fights where the other person's words burn right into you, where apologies don't keep them from scarring. But I didn't want to think about that now. So even though all the details threatened to rise up and run through my head again, I squashed them down. I focused on trying to find out what had happened, whether she was really dead.

I had an old black-and-white TV in my room. "Museum quality," my brother Tom always joked, but it was good enough to get me the eleven o'clock news. Yes, there had been an accident on Black Mountain Road. They showed the car, gnarled metal that looked like it could've once been Pam Henderson's car. One fatality, the passenger. The driver had been taken to the hospital. No names were being released yet.

One fatality, the passenger. I knew then. But some part of me didn't believe it, and in the days after that I kept waiting for more information, waiting for the story to change. Even when everybody knew she was dead, when the obituary came out and the funeral was scheduled, I kept expecting to see her in town, at school, at the bridge. Late at night, I'd call her cell number just to hear her voice in that recorded message. It took a few weeks for her parents to cut off the service. Every time I called, I was scared somebody in her family would answer the phone, but they never did.

Rumors about the accident filled the school halls. People said Julia was drunk that night but Pam wasn't. Pam came out of the accident with a broken arm and a concussion. She supposedly told her friends that Julia wasn't strapped in because she kept leaning out the window to throw up. I wasn't a friend of Pam's, so I never heard anything firsthand.

They said Pam went so crazy over the whole thing, seeing Julia die and all, that they shipped her off to a different school this year. I didn't know how much of that was true, about Pam going crazy, but she wasn't at the funeral. I managed to go; you didn't need an invitation for that. Nobody asked me what I was doing there because so many kids from school had come, even people who hardly knew Julia. I stayed in the back.

Austin was there. Julia told me she was going to break up with him at the party, but she'd said that before. If she did break up with him, he sure didn't show it. He stood with her family, held her mother's hand, patted her brother's shoulder. He went up to put a rose on her casket right after her mother did. He even stroked the surface of the casket like it was Julia's skin.

I knew Julia, but nobody else knew that. We were good at keeping secrets. So after Labor Day weekend, I was the only one who knew about us.

chapter 2

At school I always hung out with the same guys, all of us from the flats. Nick drove us in his car, now that we were juniors and could park in the good spaces in the north parking lot. We had to wait until the third week for him to take us, though, because his mother caught him drinking at the end of the summer and took away his keys for a while.

Nick and Paul sat up front, as usual. I was squished in the back with Syd and Fred. My legs took up so much room that Syd had to sit on my lap. As Nick zoomed around the curve that led into the center of town, showing off, I said, "How about giving us a chance to reach our senior year?"

"You can drive from all the way back there, huh, Morrissey?" he said. "Pretty damn good for someone without a license."

"Ten points for that squirrel," Paul said.

"You didn't really hit a squirrel, did you?" Syd asked.

"No." Nick laughed.

Blood rushed through my body, surging from one side to the other as Nick whipped us around corners. I swallowed to keep my stomach where it belonged. The heat of our bodies crammed together didn't help. We reached school just in time, as far as I was concerned. Another mile and I would've been showing everybody what I had for breakfast.

Usually I wasn't the carsick type. But I couldn't stop thinking about Julia's head exploding as it slammed into the windshield of Pam's car. Thinking and trying not to think, wondering if she felt it or if she was too drunk to know what hit her.

Julia's brother, Michael, was a sophomore. I hadn't said twenty words to him in my life, so I wasn't expecting him to speak up behind me in the cafeteria line. I hadn't seen him back there. "You're Colten Morrissey, right?" he said.

I swung my head around when he spoke. My skin prickled. If I hadn't already known who he was, I might have guessed. The ghost of Julia looked out of his eyes, was there in the bones of his face. He was skinnier than she had been, though—scrawny, even. He wore glasses, and his chin jutted out more. And while her hair had been a reddish brown, his was much darker.

"Yeah," I said. "Why?"

"I was wondering." He took something wrapped in a tortilla that our cafeteria called a "quesadilla," and put it on his tray. "You had a few classes with my sister, didn't you?"

"Uh, yeah, when I was a freshman." What had made him connect me with Julia?

He plunked a bowl of vanilla pudding onto his tray. I took a plate of something without looking at it and slid my tray along the rails.

"Which classes? Math, I believe? With Bruckner?"

"Calvert."

He snapped his fingers. "Calvert. That's right." We stopped at the drink station. He took a glass and held it under the juice spout. I watched red liquid trickle out for a minute and then forced myself to get a glass of water.

"Was Carlos Mendez in that class, too?" he said.

"Mendez? No."

"Oh."

Why the hell was he asking all this? I waited for him to explain, but he just watched his juice pour as if he'd never seen anything so fascinating. "It's almost empty," he muttered, as the flow slowed to a dribble.

"Michael—"

He looked up at me. "You came to the funeral, didn't you?"

"Yes."

"That was nice of you. Considering you didn't know her very well." I just stood there, and he moved around me to the cashier. I followed him then, an electric hum in my brain, a queasy heat rising up from my stomach. I didn't know exactly what he was after, but I didn't like it. After he'd paid for his own lunch, he waited for me to finish with the cashier. I saw him waiting and wished he'd get lost—sink through the floor, fly out the window, anything. But he was still there when I got through the line.

"You can stop squirming," he said. "I'm not going to tell anyone."

Shit. I kept my face blank. "Not going to tell anyone what?"

He gave me a thin smile and shook his head. "Are you going to play stupid now? When I mentioned my sister, you panicked."

"I don't—"

"Maybe nobody else would notice, but I can read faces." He sipped his juice. "Besides, you've just confirmed a few other things for me." He glanced around, but there was no one near us. "I know about the letters. I know you're C.M."

This time I could honestly say, "Michael, I don't know what the hell you're talking about."

"Well, I don't believe that, but never mind." He stared at me as if he could peel off my skin with his eyes. "I have something for you from my sister. If you're interested, meet me outside the east entrance after school." He took his tray to a table in the corner without giving me another look.

I went to my usual table, numb. *I know about the letters.* What letters? He obviously knew something about Julia and me, or thought he did, but whatever code he was speaking, I didn't get it. I had no idea what he wanted to give me, either. A picture of Julia? A lock of her hair? A punch in the face?

I made sure not to look over at the table of Black Mountain royalty, where Austin Chadwick sat, where Julia used to sit. I had gotten so used to avoiding her at school that now I avoided even the spaces she should have filled. But today I had another reason; I didn't want them to see whatever Michael Vernon had supposedly seen on my face.

I checked out the rest of my table to see if anyone else thought I was easy to read. Syd picked through her salad as if checking for bugs. Fred was trying to do his homework for his afternoon classes. Paul wasn't there—probably making out with his girlfriend behind the school. Nick leaned over and gawked at the sandwich on my tray.

"What is that, turkey?"

"I guess."

"You shoulda got the roast beef." He lifted his own sandwich, mayo oozing out onto his fingers.

"Something wrong, Colt?" Syd asked.

"Like what?"

She shrugged. "I don't know. You look a little off. Like you're having second thoughts about the turkey."

I shoved Michael and Julia to the back of my mind. "I'm not sure it *is* turkey." I poked the sandwich. "It's more of a turkeylike substance."

"Good point," she said, and went back to her salad.

I took a breath. "I can't ride home with you guys today," I told Nick.

"What, you got detention?"

"Yeah."

"Well," he said, grinning around a mouthful of roast beef, "enjoy the bus." And none of them gave any sign that they knew I was lying.

I didn't hear anything that went on in my afternoon classes. The teachers could've scheduled three tests for the next day, and I wouldn't have known it. All I did was watch the clock hands creep around to the final bell.

Michael was waiting for me, right where he'd said. He smiled grimly. "So, you've decided you did know Julia after all."

I didn't answer.

He pulled something out of his backpack and held it up: a purple notebook with a diagonal black stripe across its cover.

"What's that?" I asked.

"Come on. I know you're C.M."

"I'm what?"

"*C.M.* The C.M. she wrote all these letters to."

Letters? I couldn't stop staring at that book. Julia used to write me short notes sometimes ("Meet me at the bridge tonight"), always unsigned, slipped through the vent in my locker. But I didn't know anything about any letters.

"I put the clues together," he said. "It wasn't difficult. She mentioned that you lived on the flats, near Higgins Farm Bridge. She also wrote that you were younger than she was, and that you'd been in Calvert's class with her." He paused to adjust his glasses. "The only other person it could have been was Carlos Mendez, and I've ruled him out."

I wanted to know what was in that notebook, but he was only holding it up, not handing it over. For a second, I wondered if he might not even show it to me, just hold it over my head. Not that he had a reputation for that kind of viciousness, but he was definitely strange.

Nobody could figure Michael out or predict what he might do. Julia had told me a few things about him: He'd painted the ceiling of his room black. He'd taken pictures of potatoes for his freshman art project. He'd once fasted for a week as part of a report on Gandhi. I also remembered that he'd tried to start an ethics and philosophy club at school last year, but he couldn't get anyone to join. None of those facts helped me guess what he was up to now.

"You've really never seen this book before?" he asked.

"No."

"But you knew my sister." It wasn't a question. His eyes nailed me to the wall, reminding me of an old insect collection my science teacher had once shown us, bugs splayed out and frozen with pins.

"Yes," I said. It was the first time I'd admitted it to anyone.

He handed me the notebook. "Then you might as well look."

I opened it to the first page. It was Julia's, all right: black ink on lavender pages, each word bold and dark, the same writing I used to find on notes in my locker.

> Dear C.M.,
>   I had to write this down because I don't believe what just happened.

I recognized the date: the first night I'd ever met her at the bridge, last September.

I closed the book because I didn't want to read more in front of him. "Why are you showing this to me?"

"I thought about throwing it away," he said. "Burning it, pretending it never existed. But I know what Julia would've wanted. She—" He cut himself off, and swallowed. "Well. Read it if you want. I believe that's why she wrote it." He turned and walked away. He was halfway across the school lawn before I realized I probably should've thanked him.

chapter 3

Alone in my room that afternoon, I placed the notebook on my bed and stared at it for a minute. It wasn't that I was debating whether to read it. I knew I was going to read it. But at the same time, I was scared. What the hell had she written?

I flipped open the cover.

> Dear C.M.,
>   I had to write this down because I don't believe what just happened. If anyone had told me this morning that we would do what we did down by the bridge, I would've thought they were crazy. But it happened. Maybe that's why I want to write about it. I need to make it real.
>   I didn't even notice you much last year,

when you were in Calvert's class. You sat
in the back and kept your mouth shut. But
tonight it felt like you could see right into
me, like you knew what I was going to say
next. That never happens with Austin. What
I have with him doesn't go far enough.

I have to break up with him now. All I
want is to be back with you, standing thigh-
deep in the river, feeding you my tongue.

I closed the book. She had a pretty good way of describing that
first time we kissed. That didn't surprise me, since I knew she liked
to write. She wrote poems, and she'd even shown me some. Most of
them were about her family or nature or something like that, poems
she could hand in or publish in the school magazine. There were a few
poems that she showed to me but not to her English teacher. Poems
about nights we spent together. Why hadn't she ever shown me this
notebook, though? She was supposedly writing to me, after all.

"Standing thigh-deep in the river, feeding you my tongue." I
couldn't get that phrase out of my head now. That's the way it happened, all right.

That night I'd been on one of my rambles, walking along the
riverbank from where it ran behind my house down to the bridge.
Higgins Farm Road was just a two-lane street, its bridge nothing
more than a low-railinged bump in the road. They should've made
the bridge higher; it flooded every time we had a storm. It made a
good meeting place because everyone knew where it was, and when

you went under it you were out of sight of the road. And there were streetlamps, so it was never totally dark.

Kids did party there sometimes, and they had marked the bridge's underside with so much spray paint that you couldn't read any of it anymore. But most partiers liked the vacant lots on Oldgate Road better. That was especially true when the riverbank was muddy. Since it had rained a lot that week, I didn't expect to see anyone at the bridge. I had good boots, so I didn't mind the ooze and muck. In fact, I kind of liked it. Everything smelled wet.

When I got to the bridge, I saw a shiny car parked off to the side of the road. Then I noticed a girl standing up to her knees in the river. She wore a black dress, which she had hoisted up so she could wade deeper.

"What are you doing?" I called out. Ordinarily, I would've left without letting her see me. I didn't feel much like talking to anyone that night. But this was so strange—a girl wading into the river all alone in a fancy party dress—that I figured I should speak up. In case she was trying to drown herself or something.

She looked over her shoulder at me. The dress had a low back, and her white skin was the same color as the moon. "Who the hell wants to know?" She laughed.

I recognized her then. I knew a lot of Black Mountain kids by sight, even if we never talked, because they were in some of my classes. She was a year older than me, but she'd been in my math and science classes. "You going swimming, Julia?"

"Sure." She kicked up a foot, spraying drops. "Who are you?" She squinted at me. "Oh, I know you. You were in my math class last year. But I don't remember your name."

"Colt Morrissey."

"Right. You live around here?" She swept out an arm like she was welcoming me to the neighborhood, like it was perfectly normal to be standing in the Willis River in the middle of the night.

"Yeah. But you don't. What are you doing here?" She'd let go of her dress, and the bottom of it dragged in the water. "You always wear that to come wash your feet?"

She ran her hands down the top of her dress, the sides of her hips, her thighs. "You like black satin? I thought it would be nice for a dip in the river."

"Okay. Just so you're not drowning yourself or anything." I hadn't meant to say it that bluntly, but after talking to her for a couple of minutes I still had no idea what she was doing, and it made me nervous.

"Drown myself? Over Austin Chadwick?" Her laugh made me shiver—something about the way it tore out of her throat, like it shouldn't be a laugh at all. "Yeah, that'll happen."

I didn't know what to say. I didn't want to hear about Chadwick. I figured that she'd come here to cool off after having a fight with him. "Your dress is getting wet."

"I could take it off." She smirked, but when I didn't say anything, her mouth softened. "You know, when I said that, your eyes didn't even bug out of your head. I like that." She held out a hand. "Come join me?"

"In the water?"

"Well, that's where I am."

I don't know why I did it. I took off my boots, because they were good boots and I didn't want to fill them with river water. I took off my socks, too. Then I waded out to her. My jeans got soaked and heavy, clinging to my legs. "Happy now?"

She couldn't stop laughing. "I can't believe you did it."

"Why not?" My toes sank into the velvety silt floor of the river. It felt slick, oily. I hoped we wouldn't step on any of the broken glass or rusted cans I sometimes found here. Looking down at her legs, I said, "Aren't you worried about leeches?"

She shrugged. "They don't hurt. I'd just peel them off."

I'd never thought a princess from Black Mountain would say anything like that. That was when I started to like her.

We stood a few feet apart. The river swirled gently around our legs. "What are you doing down here?" she asked. "You always come to the bridge at night?"

"Night, daytime, whenever." It was none of her business what I was doing here. "I like it here."

"This town isn't that big," she said. "There can't possibly be *two* of us who just like to come look at the river at night."

"Then what do you think I'm doing? Meeting my fellow secret agents? Passing them my latest surveillance notes?"

She laughed and scooped up a handful of black water. "It's like liquid ebony," she said, and it ran through her fingers. "There was this dance tonight up at the country club. Austin got drunk. He thinks it's fun to spend five hours hanging over a toilet bowl." She shook her wet hand, spraying me with drops of the river. "I mean, God, when he gets drunk I can't even *talk* to him! He can't follow a conversation. He can't kiss without slobbering."

"Austin the Teenage Alcoholic," I said. "It would make a great TV movie."

"Ohhh, listen to that sarcasm. You don't like him."

"Why should I like him?"

She shrugged. "You're right. There's no reason you should." She turned away from me, and the breeze caught her hair. "Anyway, it's not like I've never been drunk myself. But there's a difference between a little buzz and all-out drooling sloppy."

"Don't worry," I said. "If he needs it, I'm sure his daddy will buy him a new liver."

She turned back around. I thought maybe I'd gone too far with that one, and she'd slap me or something, but she grinned instead. "You think he's got everything, don't you?"

That one didn't even need an answer.

"Colt," she said, teasing, scolding. "If you're lucky, you should *know* you're lucky."

That was exactly how I'd always felt about the people who lived on Black Mountain. But I'd never put it into words before, or heard anyone else put it into words. "You talking about Austin?"

"I'm talking about you."

"Me?"

"You don't believe it? You need me to tell you how?" She stepped closer to me. "I could go with the obvious, tell you how someone sleeping on the street would be glad to live in your house. Or how a ninety-year-old with a walker would love to be seventeen like you."

"Sixteen," I interrupted. I wanted to choke myself as soon as I said it. It wasn't even exactly true; at that point I was still a couple of weeks shy of sixteen. Why did I have to remind her I was younger than she was?

"Whatever. But I won't even go that basic. I can tell you how you're luckier than Austin Chadwick."

"This ought to be good."

She took another couple of steps toward me, close enough now that I could smell her shampoo, a soapy peach scent that I got to know very well later. She counted on her fingers. They were long and white, with perfectly curved nails. I wanted to touch them, but I didn't. "One, you're smarter than Austin. Two, you're probably *not* an alcoholic. Three, you're better looking than he is. Four, you've got the balls to wade out into the Willis River with me."

"That's some list."

She laughed low in her throat and took one more step, and now I could feel the heat coming off her skin. "You still think Austin has it better than you? You'd rather be sprawled out on the floor of the country club men's room than here with me?"

"Not especially."

That's when she kissed me.

I'd had a girlfriend the year before—Jackie—my first real girl-friend. She'd moved away over the summer. We'd done everything together, but the first time I kissed Julia, I felt like I hadn't done any-thing. Julia's mouth was hot and the river was cold and her satin dress was so smooth it didn't even seem to be there.

"Five," she said, breathing hard, "you're a much better kisser than Austin."

chapter 4

I didn't really believe all that stuff Julia had said about me being better at kissing than Austin. I figured she was just mad at him, and horny, and I happened to be there, so what the hell.

Nick once argued with the rest of us guys about whether girls get horny the way guys do. Nick said they didn't. I said they did. To prove my point, I told him about the time Jackie dragged me into the toolshed in her backyard. Her family was having a barbecue, and her relatives were all over the place, but she pulled me into the dark shed and undid my belt. The place smelled of lawnmower gas and mildew, but we didn't care. We knocked spiderwebs off a lawn-chair cushion and did it right there. It wasn't like I fought her off, but she definitely made the first move. I never would've have tried to jump her in the middle of her family picnic.

Jackie blew a gasket when it got back to her that I'd told Nick about that day. She didn't talk to me for a week. And she was right that I should've kept my mouth shut; I wasn't as good at keeping secrets back then as I became later. But it was true that she liked sex as much as I did, so I assumed it was true for Julia, too. Especially when I remembered the way she'd kissed me at the river.

Anyway, the Monday after I first saw Julia at the bridge, I didn't think she would come walking up to me at school, and she didn't. I figured she'd probably never talk to me again. I wasn't expecting to find a note in my locker: "Meet me at the bridge tonight, 9:30."

I wondered if it could be a joke. Or a setup: I'd go down to the bridge and find Austin Chadwick and his friends waiting to knock my teeth out. But somehow I knew it was real, even though I didn't see her at school all day. It was like we'd gotten tuned to each other from just one meeting. And at nine-thirty, I went down to the river.

That night she wore regular clothes, jeans and a white shirt. No more black satin. She was sitting on the hood of her car, waiting for me. I walked up to her.

"So you are real," she said. "I thought I must've dreamed Friday night."

"How did you know which locker was mine?"

"I work in the office on my study period, for extra credit. I can look up anybody's locker." She grinned. "Morrissey, Colten, 238A."

"Congratulations."

She moved over to let me sit down, but I hesitated. I could imagine myself scratching that showroom-fresh finish. Then she said, "Get up here," so I did.

"I'm not planning to swim tonight," she said. "But you go ahead if you want to."

"No swimming? I guess you only wear your black dress for that."

"Except when I wear my silver dress, with the tiara."

"You don't really *have* a tiara, do you?"

She laughed. "No, do you?"

"Only five or six."

I let silence fall between us and lie there. It wasn't completely quiet; I could hear crickets and the lapping of the river against the shore. I wanted to touch her but felt like I didn't have the right.

"That's amazing," she said at last.

"What?"

"That you can stand silence. Austin can't take much quiet. Neither can any of my other friends. It's like they're afraid to have time to think."

I liked the way we slid from laughing to serious, from talking to quiet and back again. I could've sat there all night with her, letting things flow that way. But something made me push, made me ask, "So why did you want me to come down here?"

"I—" She closed her mouth and thought for a minute. "I wanted to see you again."

"Where's Austin?"

She winced. "Don't ask me about Austin, okay?"

"Then what the hell are we doing here?"

"Well . . . I'm open to suggestions."

I didn't like her smirk when she said that. It wasn't that I minded her flirting with me. I just didn't believe that I could be with her tonight without some catch, some price tag. I thought of the way fish get hooked, the metal biting into their mouths, drawing blood.

"God, Colt!" She laughed. "You should see your face. Don't you trust me?"

"Why should I?"

She put her hand on the front of my shirt, leaned toward me. I could've pulled away but I didn't. I met her halfway for the kiss and it was as good as it had been the other night. Maybe better. "Remember this?" she whispered.

"Yeah, I remember. So you want a replay of the other night?"

"Except I don't want to stop this time."

My pulse jumped. But I said, "And then what happens?" I could almost feel the hook sinking into the roof of my mouth.

She pulled back. "I don't know. Do you need to think that far ahead?"

"Yes."

Her bottom lip fell a bit, and she laughed. "I never know what you're going to say next."

I waited.

"Well, let's see," she said to an imaginary audience. "Colt wants to know what is going to happen after tonight. Now, the world could explode, but probably not. Or we could discover the portal to another universe, but probably not that either."

"I'm just asking what you want from me, seeing how you already have a boyfriend."

"Come on, Colt, what do *you* want? You want to be my boyfriend and come to the country club, and have dinner with my parents, and sit with my friends at lunch? Or would you rather meet me here nights and let the rest of the world go to hell for a while?"

She wasn't really offering the boyfriend role, I knew, but she was right that I wouldn't have wanted it. Not that way, not putting on the Austin suit and stepping into his shoes. "So you want to meet me here nights," I said. "No strings. Fine with me."

"Isn't it better this way?" Coaxing, as if she were trying to soothe my supposedly hurt feelings, her hand on my thigh now.

"Julia, it doesn't matter to me. You can go back up on Black Mountain right now, for all I care."

She snickered. Any time I thought I was going to make her mad, she laughed instead. "You're going to do that whenever you get pissed at me, right? Drag Black Mountain in between us, like a big old shield."

She saw through me; I had to admit it. "Yeah," I said, "this way I'll never be wrong. Everybody knows rich people are the evil ones."

We laughed together. And then she led me into the backseat of her car.

I wondered what had happened between the first entry in Julia's notebook, when she wrote that she had to break up with Austin, and the Monday night when she came up with the arrangement that we had until she died. Why had she decided to stay with him? I read the second entry in her book, which was written on the Sunday before she slipped that note into my locker.

> Dear C.M.,
>   I wish I could be strong enough to
> dump Austin. He's coming over tonight and

I can't stand the thought of stretching my face to smile, smile, smile, when all I can think about is you. And then he'll be pawing and clawing me. I guess you don't want to hear about that, but how do I know I can trust you, after one night? It was so good talking with you, touching you. I thought I was going to melt all over you. How do I know it would be like that again, though?

I started this journal because it seemed like I'd found the beginning of something with you, but now I'm not so sure. At least I know Austin, I know what I'm going to get with him. I don't know you, even if it feels like I do. I can't stop thinking about you, but maybe you're just a dream.

I closed the notebook on that.

Michael Vernon didn't mention the journal to me—or to anyone else, as far as I could tell. He sort of nodded at me sometimes in the halls, but neither of us spoke.

I read some of Julia's letters every day while September turned into October. She had written about everything: exams and grades, fights with her parents, her obsession with getting into Harvard. She described my sixteenth birthday, which we'd celebrated in the back-seat of her car. (My seventeenth had passed in a numb haze, a week after her funeral.) She wrote about driving around alone at night and how she liked to lie in bed listening to the radio. She wrote poems full of black water and jagged edges and lightning. She described some of the nights we'd had together, the swampy smell of the river and the heat of my skin on hers, the cramped steaminess of her backseat and the way we used our coats for blankets when the weather turned cold.

There were times when I wanted to plunge through the whole thing without stopping, wolf down page after page, race to the final entry. I had looked ahead, and I knew that she'd written these letters right up to the day she died.

But I couldn't take it. I could only hear so much of her voice, could only spend so long reliving the feel and scent and taste of her, before something in me filled up and I had to close the book. Some days I didn't open it at all.

I lived two Octobers at the same time: the one around me and the one in my head, the one I'd shared with Julia. Sometimes I'd get them confused and I'd expect to see her at the river, scooping handfuls of orange leaves from the riverbank and showering me with them, the way she'd done the year before. This fall had grayer, colder days. When I walked in the icy spitting rain after reading her letters about starry nights, it seemed like more than a year had passed since then.

At the end of October, I dreamed about Julia for the first time since she'd died. In my dream, she stood in the front entryway at school, just inside the glass doors. Sunlight streamed over her. I don't know why I dreamed about her in the light, since most of the time I had spent with her was in the dark. Anyway, she stood there smiling at me like nothing was wrong. I said, "They told me you were dead!"

She laughed and said, "You'll believe anything, won't you?"

And then I woke up, before I could get over the shock of seeing her again.

That week I saw Austin Chadwick walking with his arm around Emily Barrett. For the first couple of weeks of school, people had treated Austin like a victim of terminal illness. They practically whispered when they talked to him; gentleness oozed from every pore. But that had worn off, and now nobody paid any special attention to Austin. The fact that he was with Emily didn't seem to shock anyone but me. I wondered what Julia would've thought.

chapter 5

My whole week used to build up to Friday. The juices gathered, the heat and pressure rose, set to erupt on schedule. It didn't matter that I got off by myself during the week. At most, that just shaved a little off the edge, kept me from boiling over. I was always ready for Friday night.

Back then I didn't have too hard a time shaking Nick and Syd and the others when I wanted to go meet Julia. They knew I spent a lot of time alone. If I didn't hang out with them, they figured I was just walking by the river or vegging in front of the TV.

Julia's life was trickier. She often canceled our Fridays, or switched the days around, because of country-club parties she couldn't get out of, or dances, or somebody's birthday. Sometimes she had me meet her as late as eleven o'clock, after she'd already gone somewhere else. When she moved the day, it screwed with my hormones, but I managed. It could be even more exciting when we had to scramble to find a way to meet.

I didn't ask what excuses she gave Austin, because I never liked to bring up his name, but once she told me anyway. She said she kept things simple, didn't invent complicated stories that could trip her up. She'd say, "Look, I just need to be alone. It's not like we're married," and he'd back off. He went out drinking with Keith Groome and Adam Hancock and his other friends while she was with me.

Now Fridays were flat; the whole week was flat. Sometimes I couldn't believe I'd had any other life besides reading a dead girl's words and watching rain beat brown leaves off the trees. Even when I went out with Syd and the guys, I had to force myself to bring my brain along. I was always half a step behind, missing the jokes, forgetting to listen. I didn't drink with them because I wasn't sure what I might say drunk, if I would spill something stupid. It was easier to stay home alone with the notebook or walk by the river.

But on the first Friday in November, I finally had a mission, something to look forward to. I went home right after school so I could catch my mother before she left for work. She had the four-to-midnight shift at Barney's Family Steakhouse. I found her sitting at the kitchen table, in her uniform, smoking a cigarette. Her feet were up on one of the chairs.

"Well, look who decided to drop by," she said. "I figured you're still living here, since food goes missing from the fridge, and I keep finding the bathroom door locked with Niagara Falls pounding away in there, but I couldn't be completely sure. Sometimes I forget what you look like." She squinted at me through the smoke. "Grew another three inches, didn't ya?"

"I don't know." I was getting tall, that was true. In the backseat of Nick's car, I never had enough room for my knees. "You didn't forget about tomorrow, did you?"

"It's all that milk you drink," she went on, as if I hadn't said a word. "At least I *hope* it's you who's going through that half gallon a day, plus all the cereal, and peanut butter, and roast beef, and apples, and potato chips, and bananas, and ham, and cookies—"

"I don't drink a half gallon a day." Mom loved to exaggerate. "Did you remember about tomorrow?"

"—because if it's not you, we've got a pretty hungry ghost on our hands." You couldn't stop one of my mother's rants; I don't know why I bothered trying. She stubbed out her cigarette and sighed. I guess she'd run out of things to say about my appetite, because she finally answered my question. "Yeah, I remember tomorrow. That's all I need, hell on wheels. Did you study the manual? Because I'm not driving you all the way down there and have you flunk the test."

I'd had to wait until my brother left home to try for my driver's license because my mother didn't want to insure two teenagers on her car. One was expensive enough, she said. And so I would be the last guy in my group to make that magical trip to the DMV. "Yes, I studied. I passed driver's ed. I'm all set. Want to leave at nine?"

"Nine in the morning? Well, if you can get up that early on a Saturday when you feel like it, I've got plenty of chores you can do on Saturday mornings. . . ."

I opened the refrigerator.

"There he goes again. Colt, would you do us a favor and leave some crumbs for dinner?"

"Remember, when I have my license, I can bring in some money." Mom had a job lined up for me at the steakhouse, busing tables. I would start Sunday if I passed the driver's test.

She cackled. "Groceries. Uh-huh. That's the first thing you'll spend your paycheck on, right?"

"I will if it'll shut you up about how much I eat." I sat down at the table with a hunk of cheese, a box of crackers, and a bowl of grapes.

She got to her feet, groaning. Her legs were always hurting her. "Come Sunday, you can start your own crop of varicose veins."

After she left, I was glad to sit in the quiet. My dad wasn't home. He was a tiler who only worked now and then. He might've been out on a job, but he was probably out drinking. I was a little sorry I'd hassled my mother about the license. I knew I couldn't count on my father, though, and I wanted that card. Not only would it mean more freedom for me, but it would be the one new thing that had happened since Julia's death. In the two months since Labor Day, that night had been sitting in the bottom of my stomach. I'd been stuck in some time-dead zone where everything was the same, day after day, and none of it was good. Something had to change. Anything.

Syd called later while I was in bed, watching some old rerun on TV. "Good luck tomorrow," she said.

"Thanks."

"If you get your license, you want to take me for a ride tomorrow night?"

"Sure. If I can get the car." Syd's parents wouldn't let her drive until she was eighteen. They always treated her as younger than she was, made her wait longer for things than anyone else had to wait.

"I wish we could go out tonight," she said. "I can't stand it here."

"What's wrong?"

"Oh, my parents had another fight, and they haven't talked all night. Do you know what it's like to be in a house with two people who won't speak to each other?"

Actually, I did. I'd been at Syd's house during some of those freeze-outs. You wouldn't think two people not talking could fill a house, but my mother's yelling was never as loud as their silence.

"You can come over here if you want," I said. "Tom's bed is free."

"Thanks, but they'd never let me out of the house at this hour."

"Yeah, I guess you're right."

"What are you doing?" she asked after a long pause.

"Watching a stupid show."

"What channel?"

I told her, and she switched her TV to the same channel. We sat there watching the same show, not talking much, neither of us wanting to hang up.

When I finally got off the phone, I looked over at the desk where I kept Julia's notebook. I didn't need to hide it since nobody came into my room. Watching TV with Syd had relaxed me, and I really didn't want to look at those letters tonight. Sometimes reading the notebook had the same effect on me that Julia herself used to have. I'd come back from seeing her, feeling like I'd had an electric jolt, wanting to tell someone about the night we'd had. Then the next minute I'd want to keep it between the two of us forever. With Julia, I always seemed to want opposite things at the same time. She stirred me up, and tonight I didn't want to get stirred up.

I shut off the light.

My dad and his friends were out in the yard, looking over the wrecks, when Mom and I left the next morning. Sometimes they'd scavenge for parts. Other times they'd stand around bullshitting about the cars they'd once owned and the cars they would buy if they had the money. I never joined them unless Dad forced me to, because I was only interested in vehicles that actually had a chance to get me somewhere.

The guys stood in a circle, smoking and talking. "Hey, Tommy!" one of them yelled at me.

"No, that's the other one. The younger one," Dad told him. Because I didn't spend much time with them, I wasn't surprised they couldn't tell me from my brother. Even though Tom had curly hair and freckles like Mom, and I had straight hair like Dad.

As she drove me over to the DMV, Mom said, "Now don't smash into anything during the test."

"Thanks for the tip. Because I was planning to crash into a couple of things."

"And make sure you put on your seat belt and check your mirrors. They look for any little thing like that to trip you up."

"Uh-huh."

"And signal when you change lanes," she said, swerving into the passing lane. Without signaling.

"If I pass the test, can I take the car tonight?"

"Already? Christ."

"Just to celebrate. After this, I'll pretty much be taking it to work and back."

"Celebrate, huh. The cops'll be peeling you off a tree."

"Cheer up. Maybe I'll hit a guardrail instead." In the middle of arguing with my mother, I'd actually forgotten about Julia for five minutes. As soon as we started talking about car crashes, though, I remembered. Not that I knew whether Pam and Julia had hit a tree, or a guardrail, or something else. I'd managed not to know the exact details. But thinking about it made my breakfast roll into a ball and try to push itself back up my throat.

"Yeah, keep up that attitude. Those DMV guys love a smart-ass."

I swallowed down the breakfast along with thoughts of Julia, and the accident, and everything else I would rather forget. I flipped open the driver's manual and pretended to study the rules I'd already read about five hundred times. At least Mom left me alone while I was reading.

I spent the morning mostly waiting in lines while my mother sat on a plastic chair reading *People* magazine. "Aren't you done yet?" she'd ask, every time I reported back to her after making my way through another line (written test, eye exam, road test, picture). Finally, license in hand, I could say yes.

"Want me to drive home?" I asked her.

"You think my heart can take it?"

"Now who's being a smart-ass?"

"Watch your mouth." She smacked the side of my face. "Okay, you can drive, but if you crash the car you're paying for it."

"I love the way you *believe* in me."

She grunted.

I got us out of the lot and onto the main road without anything going wrong. The two-lane road went straight through fields that used to be farmlands. Every year while I was growing up, more of the houses had boards over their windows and skinny trees growing in their driveways. Tom and I played in some of those houses when we were younger. We would pry off a board and slip inside, tiptoe through the empty rooms where only mice lived anymore. I used to wonder if the flats would eventually turn into a ghost town. But now there were new developments edging in, treeless tracts of identical houses with golf-course grass. These new places had names like "Floral Meadows" and "Riverview Estates," which made my brother laugh every time we drove by them.

When Mom and I were on Route 17, Austin Chadwick's red car went screaming past us, passing on the shoulder. "Asshole," Mom muttered.

"You got that right."

"You know him?"

"He goes to my school."

"I ever catch you driving like that, I'll cut up your license and flush it down the toilet."

"How many hundreds of times are you going to tell me that?"

"I want to make sure you get it."

"I get it, I get it."

Dad and his friends were gone by the time we got home. Mom said she had to get ready for her shift. "Enjoy your last day of freedom," she said. "Tomorrow you'll be sweating for pennies with the rest of us working slobs."

"When you put it that way, I can't wait." I took a breath and said, "Thanks for coming with me."

She waved that away. "Hell, I *had* to." But I think she was glad I said it.

Syd was supposed to call me when she finished dinner, so I read more of the notebook while I waited for her. I was up to an entry from last November, written about two months after I'd started seeing Julia.

I did what I always did when I read the notebook: locked my door and shut off all the lights except the one over my bed. Not that anyone had ever walked in on me or would care if they did. But I wanted to shut out the world as much as I could when I opened this book.

> Dear C.M.,
>
> I can't stop thinking about you. I'm supposed to see Austin tonight, and I'd rather chew on sandpaper. If I have to listen to one more story about how wasted he got, or the magic chemical mixture he invented to clean a smudge off his car seats, I'll hang myself. Why do I stay with him? You never ask, but sometimes I wonder if it bothers you that I'm with him. Maybe you're even glad. It lets you off the hook. I told you once that you wouldn't want to be my boyfriend, and you didn't argue with me.

> The thing about Austin is, we have a
> lot in common. We both like dancing and
> partying, and it's fun until he gets too
> drunk. Sometimes on Sunday afternoons,
> I go to his house and the family's sitting
> around with the Sunday paper all over
> the place, and maybe we play a game or
> something, and it's nice. I belong there. With
> Austin, everything fits. With you, I never
> know.

Austin again. Julia wrote a lot about him, a lot more than I wanted to read. Sometimes her attitude seemed to be that she belonged with him, so I'd better live with it and not ask her for anything more. Other times she'd go on and on about how she'd had enough of him and really wanted to be with me—the same bullshit she'd told me at the river. Both attitudes were somewhat fake, I thought. That is, she didn't completely love Austin, but she didn't completely hate him either. I guess she stayed with him because it was easy, because it was what everyone expected of her.

There must have been some reason besides that, though, something I was missing. It was hard to believe that a girl who went swimming in a black satin dress cared about what was easy and expected.

Syd called as I was closing the notebook. "Colt? Did you get your license?"

"Yes."

She squealed. "So where are we going?"

"Wherever you want. Except I can't use up more gas than I can pay for."

"Let's drive to the top of Black Mountain."

There was a park up there, where kids went to party, or look at the view, or screw around in their cars. "What for?"

"For the view."

"At night?"

"You can see the lights."

"All right, if that's what you want."

It would be my first time up Black Mountain Road since the accident. I'd always known I would have to do it sometime. I figured it might as well be tonight.

chapter 6

Black Mountain Road wound upward beneath pines and oaks, maples and hemlocks. You couldn't see most of the houses from the road, just the gateposts at the ends of people's driveways. A lot of the houses had names. Tom and I used to joke that if we gave our own house a name, it would be "Rusty Acres" or "Swamp-side Manor."

I was glad that I didn't know exactly which curve on Black Mountain Road was *the* curve. It could've been any one of them, and there were no mangled guardrails to give me a clue. Kids had made one of those flower-and-candle roadside shrines up here for Julia, but I wasn't sure exactly where, and it had been moved down to the cemetery on Morgansfield Road after the funeral. I'd never visited it in either place. To me, that wasn't where Julia was.

I'd never taken in all the details of the accident. I hadn't wanted to picture it; I didn't want that night to live in my head. It was only now that I wanted the whole story. The notebook had cracked me open, brought back Julia's voice. It was like I still had something important to find out about her. About us.

I didn't notice I'd been holding my breath until I let it out at the top of the mountain. Syd misunderstood my sigh. She said, "See, I told you it was beautiful."

I parked facing the view. The trees of Black Mountain, a wild dark tangle, filled the slope below us. The flats spread out at the foot of the mountain in a carpet of lights.

A few other cars clustered at the far end of the lot. One streetlight stood close enough to us for me to see Syd, but not close enough to throw a real glare into the car. I wiped the windshield with my sleeve, but most of the spots were on the outside.

"Imagine seeing this out your bedroom window," Syd said, gazing at all those lights where there used to be nothing but farms. "I wonder what it's like to live up here."

"I wouldn't know."

"Do you think they even notice it? To them it's probably ordinary."

"Probably." I'd been to Julia's house a couple of times when nobody else was home. Her room didn't face the view—her windows looked out onto pine trees—and I couldn't remember looking out any of the other windows. I had crept through the place like a burglar, trying not to leave fingerprints anywhere. I didn't belong there.

"I'm going to live up here someday." Syd stared as if she could take hold of the mountain, and all the land around it, with her eyes.

"Not me," I said. "I'd rather live on the river."

"Well, I'll live up here and you can come visit sometimes."

"Sounds good." I figured she was only dreaming, but the practical details nagged at me. "How would you make that kind of money, though?"

"I think . . ." She licked her lips. "If I tell you something, promise not to tell Nick and the other guys?"

"Sure."

"I think I want to be a doctor. The kind that takes care of little kids, you know?"

"Why does that have to be a secret?"

"Oh, the guys would make fun of me. Remember how Nick was when your brother got into college? Anyway, I don't know if I could make it. It costs a ton of money."

"You'd be good at it." When I was eight and cut my hand on a broken bottle, Syd was the only kid in my class who could look at the stitches without flinching.

"I talked about it to Mr. Morea, and he said, 'You know you have to cut up a cadaver in medical school.' Then he stared at me like he expected me to faint or something."

"So what'd you say?"

"I said, 'Yeah, I know, but what worries me is the money. How am I going to pay for eight years of school?'"

I laughed. I would've loved to see Morea's face when she said that. He was always trying to rattle her. People underestimated Syd because she was quiet and small, and she usually wore a big old jacket of her father's that made her look even smaller. You'd think Morea would know better by now. When we first used microscopes in his class, he insisted on leaning over Syd and working the knobs for her, like it was too complicated for her to figure out. She finally told him, "You're putting it out of focus," and flicked his hands away.

"I bet you could get a scholarship," I said.

"Maybe."

"You could. You've got the grades for it."

Syd shrugged and went quiet.

I rubbed the steering wheel. The cracks in its cover caught on the skin of my hands. I stroked the smooth patch where my mother had wrapped black tape around one of the first cracked spots. She no longer bothered patching the wheel; she said the whole thing would be covered in tape.

I liked the feel of the wheel, liked knowing all I had to do was start the car and I could go anywhere I wanted. Not that I had anyplace special to go. Just knowing I could was enough. When I looked over at Syd, staring out at the lights and dreaming about her Black Mountain future, I thought maybe she'd like that freedom, too. "Want me to teach you?" I asked.

"Teach me what?"

"To drive."

"Really?" She smiled. "No, my parents would kill me."

"Who has to tell them?"

"They would kill me," she said again, but her laugh was so excited that I took her hand and guided it to the wheel. Half teasing, half ready to hand her the keys if only she asked, I slid her hand along the steering wheel.

"See, doesn't that feel good?"

"Colt!" She pulled away and slapped my shoulder. "Don't tempt me. Me not driving is one of the few things my parents agree on."

"If you say so." I was having second thoughts myself. Mom would slaughter me if she found out I used her car to give driving lessons when I hadn't even had my license for a full day yet.

Syd sighed. "On the other hand, maybe they wouldn't notice. They're so wrapped up in their own bullshit lately." She rested her head against the back of the seat. "My dad's sleeping downstairs again."

I didn't know what to say to that. I waited for her to go on, but instead she changed the subject. "Tell me about the driver's test," she said. I told her, and then we got quiet again. A couple more cars showed up, but they parked far away from us. We were still just sitting there when someone knocked on the window. We jumped. I hadn't heard anyone walk up.

Keith Groome crouched there, looking in at us. I rolled down the window a couple of inches. He was so close I could smell the beer on his breath. I said, "What do you want?"

He sneered. "What the hell you doing up here?" When I didn't answer, he said, "White trash is supposed to stay down on the flats."

"Go to hell," I said, and rolled up the window. He banged on the glass and hollered.

"Oh God," Syd said, "let's just go."

"Why? This is a public park."

"Come on, please. I hate this."

"Relax. He'll give up."

"Well, I can't concentrate with him screaming like that."

I went for my door handle, but Syd grabbed me. "No, don't. You know I hate fights."

Groome hammered on the car roof.

"This is so stupid," Syd said. "Can we just go?"

"Okay." I started the engine. "Maybe I can run him over."

"Colt!"

Groome had already stepped away from the car by the time I put it in reverse, but instead of backing straight out, I turned the car in his direction. I wasn't really trying to run him over, but I didn't mind if I scared him a little. He picked up a rock and flung it at the car. It hit somewhere in the back; we heard the *thunk.* I rolled down the window again. "You're going to pay for that, asshole."

"Sure, here's a quarter!" he yelled.

"Just get us out of here," Syd pleaded.

I took off, forgetting to be scared as I brought us around the curves of Black Mountain Road. I pulled over near the bottom because I was beginning to think I was too mad to drive. As much as I missed Julia, I didn't want to meet her on the same stretch of road. I looked over at Syd.

"I hate it," she said. "They think they're so much better than us."

I shut off the engine and the lights and put my arms around her. "It's okay," I told her. She pressed her face into my chest.

A car came screeching down Black Mountain Road then. It flew by us, with four others right behind it. They headed toward the Higgins Farm Bridge, and I laughed.

"It's Groome and his friends," I said. "They didn't even see us!" I couldn't stop laughing. I imagined them tearing around the flats, trying to teach me a lesson, and here they had driven right *past* me.

"They make me sick," Syd said. "There's something seriously wrong with Keith Groome."

"Don't let them get to you." Even under the oversized jacket, I could feel how tense she was. I held her until her body loosened, softened. "I'll take you home now."

"Okay."

I dropped her off and drove back to my place without seeing Groome and his friends again. I checked out the back of the car with a flashlight, but I honestly couldn't find the dent Groome had made among all the other dents, dings, and scars.

I read another page in Julia's notebook as soon as I got to my room. I didn't go in order this time, but just opened the book anywhere, to a date in January. I didn't read it because I was thinking about Julia as a person. Instead, I liked knowing how pissed Groome and Austin and those guys would be if they knew I'd been with her. Opening the notebook was almost a kind of revenge. Until I read the entry.

> Dear C.M.,
>   I couldn't believe it when you didn't show up last night. I had a good fuming fit and threw a few snowballs in the river, waiting for you. Then I saw your name on the absence lists in the office. Turns out you haven't been in school for a week! So you never even got my note asking you to meet me.

Are you sick? I want to call you. I just
looked up your family's number. I'm pretty
sure it's yours because the address is on
the flats, near the Higgins Farm Bridge.
Would you want me to call you? I feel so
cut off from you. It seems crazy that I
don't even know how you are. Sometimes I
love the fact that nobody knows about us.
We have this secret, so juicy I can feel
my mouth dripping. Other times, like now, it
seems stupid to hide this way.

It's later: I just talked to you. You
didn't sound mad. Your voice felt good in
my ear. I'm glad I called.

I remembered that, all right. Last winter I got the flu, and I was
out for almost two weeks. At the end of the first week, Julia called.
I didn't have a fever anymore, but I still felt horrible, beaten up and
wrung out, not to mention bored. My brother had brought me a
bunch of library books, but I'd read them, and I'd memorized the
daytime TV schedule. Watching that much afternoon TV, I had discovered that there were about ten personal-injury lawyers who would
be thrilled to take my case, if I ever had one. And I could have an
exciting career in heating and air-conditioning. Anyway, I was lying
there in the sheets I'd sweated on, trying to work up the energy to
take a shower, when Julia called.

"Are you sick? I was worried about you," she said.

"Yeah, I've got the flu." I held the phone away so I could cough. "Sorry. I'm getting better."

"When are you coming back to school?"

"Maybe next week. I don't know. I still can't get out of bed much."

There was a long pause. I tried to hear her breathing. Then she said, "I miss you."

"I miss you, too."

We didn't say much else, though we stayed on the phone for a while longer. Her voice felt good in my ear, too.

chapter 7

On Sunday Syd and the guys came over to shoot targets. My family had a few acres of weedy muck that ran down to the river. Our land was cheap because part of it flooded every year. Twice we'd had water as far up as our house. Out back we had a bunch of different targets, and sometimes we set up cans on top of the junked cars. Dad only kept two cars behind the house; the rest were in the front. My brother Tom's "sculpture," a kind of wooden tower about twelve feet high, was in the backyard, too.

Nick was the best shot, then Syd, then me, then Paul, then Fred. I thought Syd was still shaken up from the night before, though, because she was missing everything today.

"So you finally got your license," Nick said to me, when the only one who still felt like shooting was Fred. Fred liked to practice, because he was always hoping to get better. I thought he probably needed glasses but wouldn't admit it. Anyway, Fred kept going while the rest of us sat on the back-porch steps. There was no room for us on the porch itself, what with the dead washing machine, the snow shovels, the engine parts, the half-empty cans of WD-40, and a pile of old boots.

"Yeah," I told Nick, "but I won't get to use the car much, except to go to work."

"How'd you get roped into that? Busing tables at the steakhouse. Christ."

"I don't mind. I could use the money."

"Yeah, some of us have to earn our money," Paul said, leaning back and spreading his arms along the top of the step. He pumped gas thirty-five hours a week. "Who do you think you are, Nick? Austin Chadwick, who don't gotta work for a living?"

Nick grinned. "You guys gotta learn to work the system. I told my folks they should just give me an allowance, because if I got a job it would interfere with my grades."

We all laughed at that, except Syd. "And they bought that?" Paul said. "How drunk were they?"

"Hell, no. I gave 'em the old innocent look. 'Seriously, Mom, I gotta concentrate on school.'" The blond stubble on Nick's face glinted; he rubbed it to make a raspy noise. Nick liked to go for days without shaving. He thought it made him look tough. But since he didn't have thick enough whiskers for a real beard, he would shave as soon as the hair got long and wispy.

Through all this, Syd leaned back against the step above her. She hadn't said much today. Not that she ever talked a lot, but even when Syd didn't speak she was still usually part of the conversation. Most of the time, I could tell what she was thinking. Sometimes the two of us would have our own silent conversation, just by looking at each other. But today she stared out toward the river, and I couldn't tell if she was listening to us. Aside from a squabble she'd had earlier with Nick, over which one of them was going to shoot first, she barely seemed to notice she was with us.

"You think you're Chadwick," Paul told Nick again. "Fuck, I can see you now, living up on Black Mountain—"

"How's he gonna work that?" Fred yelled.

"Move in with some old widow. Like Blankenship." Paul laughed.

"Black Mountain Gigolo!" Fred said.

"Hell, not even Blankenship would take Nick," I said. Mrs. Blankenship lived high up on Black Mountain. She was about a hundred and two, and she spent most of her time giving money to places that would name buildings after her. If she ever did go for Nick, she'd probably stamp PROPERTY OF BLANKENSHIP on him.

"I wouldn't take anyone on Black Mountain," Nick said. "They're all bitches and ugly as shit. You seen that Lori Van Allen? You can't tell her apart from that horse she's always riding."

"Julia Vernon was hot," Fred said, and turned back to the targets. It felt like ants were swarming over me. I glanced at Syd—she was the only person who might read my mind—but she was still off somewhere else. I pretended that something about my left shoelace was really interesting.

"She's dead," Nick said. "How sick are you?"

While Julia was alive, I had gotten good at covering, at keeping my face blank and my breathing steady whenever I saw her or heard anything about her. It took a while. At first, it was the little things that almost tripped me up. Like the time I went into a drugstore with Nick so he could buy cigarettes, and I remembered I needed condoms. I almost got them off the shelf before I realized I couldn't buy a box that big in front of Nick when I supposedly didn't even have a girlfriend. Or the time I had to explain to Paul how I knew before everyone else that Keith Groome's father had been arrested for a DUI. I got out of that one by saying Syd had told me . . . good thing she was known for being up on all the Black Mountain gossip.

I learned. At some point, hiding the truth became automatic. I could flip a switch inside, cross from one side of myself to the other without thinking. Then the crash had scraped me raw. The weeks right after Labor Day had been torture, with everyone gossiping about her death and girls crying in the school halls, but even then I'd gone numb from the constant buzz about it. Now I was raw again, focusing on the plastic end of my shoelace and wishing they'd change the subject to anything else.

"Pam Henderson wasn't bad," Paul said. "Nice ass."

Nick smirked at Syd. "Hey, Syd, that's your cue to tell Paul what an asshole he is, 'objectifying women' and all that."

"Fuck off, Nick," she said, flicking a pine needle from the knee of her jeans. I tried to catch her eye, but she wouldn't look at me.

Nick flinched. Syd almost never dropped the F-bomb, so she had the advantage of surprise. And Nick didn't like to be surprised. He looked around at us and raised his eyebrows in exaggerated shock. "Ooh, is it that time of the month already?"

"Leave her alone," I said.

With the same fake interest I'd had in my shoelace, we watched Fred take his next shot. All except Syd, whose eyes were still on the horizon. Nick broke the tension by asking me, "Hey, your parents home?" He liked to help himself to their beer when they weren't around.

"My dad, I think." Earlier that morning, he'd been sprawled in front of the TV in his shorts, watching some infomercial.

"Shit."

"God, Nick," Syd said. "How can you drink at this hour?"

"It's not that early. It's lunchtime."

She made a face.

"You know, you're a real pain in the ass today," Nick said. "What's with you, anyway?"

She didn't answer for a minute. Then she straightened up and said, "My father moved out this morning." She stomped down the porch steps and went to stand in the yard, a few feet away from us, looking down toward the river.

Everyone was quiet. Fred stopped shooting. Then Paul said, "Hey, it's not so bad. I've had three 'fathers' move out already." But Nick reached over and gave him a backhanded slap in the ribs.

The guys looked at me as if they expected me to say the magically right thing. I knew Syd better than any of them, but how should I know what she was going through? My parents were still together, even if they hardly talked to each other. I wished Nick would talk to Syd. His parents had gotten divorced three years ago.

"We're gonna get going," Nick said. "Ready, Fred? Syd, you coming?"

"No thanks," she said, keeping her back to us.

Fred gave her an awkward pat on the shoulder before he joined the guys again. When they had gone, I said, "I'm sorry."

She nodded without turning around. We stayed like that until she said, "Let's go down to the river."

I reached under the steps and pulled out this orange traffic cone that my dad once stole from a road-construction site. I put it on the top step of the porch. That was my family's signal that someone was out back, so no target shooting. Then Syd and I walked past the cars and the sculpture, past the targets and the berms behind them, through the weeds, down to the river path. If you followed it long enough, this path would take you to the Higgins Farm Bridge. That's how I used to go meet Julia.

Weeds rustled under our feet. Bittersweet hung from the trees, its berries shining red, the only bit of color left at this time of year. When we reached a fork in the path, Syd said, "Is the tree house still there?"

"I guess. I haven't been there for a couple of years."

Dad had helped Tom and me build the tree house. The left fork of the path Syd and I were standing on had once led to it, but now the trail was mostly overgrown. Syd took a few steps to the left and glanced back at me. "Let's go see."

I followed her until she stopped, confused. "I can't remember which tree it was anymore," she said.

"It's that big one off to the right. And the house is still there, see?"

We climbed up. The wood was damp, and softer than it used to be, but we tested each board and found only one rotten piece. We sat in the corner, smelling old wet wood and dead leaves. "Remember all those peanut-butter sandwiches?" she said.

We used to pack lunches to eat here, usually peanut butter. Somehow it seemed like an adventure. We would pretend we were stranded on an island. A couple of years after that, Nick and Paul snuck their fathers' magazines out here for us to look at. And then I guess we all got too old for the tree house.

"Am I the only girl who was ever up here?" Syd asked.

"Yeah. No, wait—Tommy brought Corrie Smith one time."

"Corrie Smith? You're kidding."

"Yeah, I think it was the first time he kissed a girl." I'd caught them, and Tom had told me he "just wanted to see what it was like." When I asked him what he thought, he shrugged and said, "I don't see what the big deal is." I laughed now, remembering that.

"What about you? Did you ever bring any girls here, Colt?"

"No." I leaned back, resting against the trunk of the tree. The damp floor was cold under my jeans.

She touched my hand then, stroked the back of it. I looked down at our hands and said, "I'm sorry about your father."

"I don't want to talk about it." She kept stroking my hand. I wanted to pull away but didn't see how I could. I told myself maybe she was just looking for comfort, even though it felt like more than that.

A strand of hair hung in her face, so I lifted my hand—the one she was touching—to brush it away. I expected that when I moved my hand it would break things up, but instead she leaned forward and kissed me.

I shouldn't have kissed her back. But I liked her—though maybe not the way she wanted. And her father had just left. So I kissed her back, and we didn't stop there.

It wasn't like with Julia at all. It was more like with Jackie; my mind flipped off in different directions. A squirrel wheezed in the tree above us, and the boards in the tree house creaked whenever the wind blew. I kept listening to things like that, and wondering what time it was and whether I had to get ready for work yet.

I don't mean that it didn't feel good to touch her, because in a way it did. It always does. I wasn't exactly suffering through it. I ran my mouth over her neck and eased my hands up under her shirt. But the whole time I had a rock in my stomach, because I knew I never should've taken things this far.

She was the first to pull away. "It's getting late," she whispered, hooking her bra.

I checked my watch. I had just enough time to get to work. "I need to take you home."

"I know." She pulled her father's jacket closer around her.

We climbed down without speaking.

■ *chapter 8* ■

The job was simple: set the tables, clear the tables. It wasn't *easy*—it wore me out—but it was simple. At Barney's Family Steakhouse, we didn't fold the napkins into fancy shapes or anything like that. We just had to get the clean cloth and dishes down as fast as we could. And we had to clear the tables even faster: dump and scrape, dump and scrape. There was always a line of customers waiting in the entry hall. Aside from being one of the few restaurants in our town, Barney's pulled people in off the interstate with a couple of giant billboards.

"If somebody asks you for butter or something," the manager, Al, told me when I first punched in, "don't just say 'okay.' Smile and say, 'Sure thing. Anything else I can do for you?'"

"All right."

"Because Barney's is a friendly, *welcoming* place. Remember that."

"All right."

I honestly couldn't say if it was a "friendly, welcoming place" or not. But between the roar of people talking and the clatter of dishes and the sound of kids yelling, it sure was a noisy place. I didn't even realize how noisy until I stepped outside at the end of my shift, and the silence made my ears ring.

I went home and collapsed on my bed. Mom came into my room and said, "So, how did you like it?"

"It's a 'friendly, welcoming place.'"

She laughed. "Poor kid, you look exhausted." She patted my head and turned to go. "Oh, Syd called," she said. "She wanted you to call her when you got home."

Shit. I'd been so busy at the restaurant, I'd been able to shove what had happened this afternoon to the back of my mind. "I'm too tired. I'll call her tomorrow." I clicked off the phone extension that was in my room, set my alarm, and went to bed.

At school, I didn't know how to act around Syd. She kept coming up and taking my hand, or sliding her arm around my waist. I'd hoped she would think of Sunday afternoon as a one-time thing, something that had happened when she was very upset. But to her, it was a beginning. Nick and the other guys teased us. Everyone seemed to know we'd gotten together this weekend.

I went along with it. I didn't know what else to do. In study hall, Syd told me about her parents' final fight, which had sent her father banging out of the house with a suitcase in each hand. "He took *my* suitcase," she said, "because he only had one of his own." What was I supposed to do, break into that story to tell her I just wanted to be friends?

I had to get out of this. It was breaking over me like a twenty-foot wave, too much, too soon. How had everything managed to get so out of control in only two days?

The truth was, I was still thinking about Julia. She'd been dead for more than two months, and she'd never really been my girlfriend to begin with. Austin had already gone out with three other girls by now. What was my problem? Was I going to end up building a shrine in the corner of my bedroom? Light candles in front of the purple notebook?

Some of the entries in Julia's book practically killed me. She agonized over whether her grades would get her into Harvard. She went on for pages about careers she wanted to try: surgeon, biochemist, lawyer, foreign correspondent. The day after I got together with Syd, I read an entry about the places Julia wanted to travel to. Some were places you'd expect, like Paris and Rome. Others were not so common, like Andorra and Kashmir and Patagonia.

One night at the river, she'd asked me if I'd ever heard of Bhutan. "Between China and India, isn't it?" I said. She said, "How come we're the only two people in this town who *know* that?" I started to tell her I was pretty sure that Mr. Tran, who taught history and geography, knew it, too, but that wasn't her point. "I want to go everywhere," she said. "Everywhere!" And now I couldn't stand thinking about the things she didn't get to do, the places she wouldn't see.

I thought maybe it would be easier to get over this if I didn't have to hide it, if I didn't have to pretend there was nothing to get over in the first place. I wished there were someone I didn't have to lie to about Julia. And then I remembered there was one person who knew the truth.

I shook off Syd at lunch on Thursday by telling her I had to ask someone about homework. I found Michael Vernon eating by himself, reading a book. His glasses made him look less like Julia, but you could still tell he was related to her. They had the same eyes. Seeing her in him made me slightly sick.

I sat across from him. He looked up, stuck a finger in his book, and said, "What?"

"Did you read that whole notebook?"

"Not the whole thing. Parts. Enough to get the general idea. To tell you the truth, there were sections I was happy to skip."

I wondered which parts he'd read, but I didn't ask. Sometimes Julia went into great detail about what we did together. I didn't need him seeing lines like "you lick invisible honey from my skin" and "you called my name at the end / I wrung that cry from your guts, your knees, your toes / deeper than anyone had ever reached inside you before." At least, if he'd seen them, I didn't want to know.

"Did anyone else see it?"

"No. My parents asked me to go through her books and notebooks. I gave them most of the poems I found. But that notebook . . . that was different."

"She never told you about us, did she?" I asked.

He shook his head.

Before I could say anything else, Kirby Matthews sat down next to Michael. Kirby was friends with Syd, but also with Black Mountain kids like Pam Henderson. I'd met Kirby in the fifth grade, when we'd built a papier-mâché dinosaur together. She'd given the first boy-girl party I ever went to, back when we thought of spin-the-bottle as major entertainment. I had always liked Kirby—she was easy to talk to—but right now I wished she'd disappear.

She reached into Michael's lunch bag and took a carrot stick. "Hi, Colt."

"Hi."

"I saw you walking down by the river yesterday," she said. "I waved, but you didn't see me."

"Where was this?"

"Near the Higgins Farm Bridge."

I'd been there, all right, but I hadn't seen anyone else. Then again, I hadn't been looking.

"I like it there," she said. "Especially now that all the partiers go to Oldgate Road instead. Do you know the stretch of river south of the bridge? That's my favorite part."

"Well, I live on the north side. I usually walk down as far as the bridge and back."

"Oh." She put her hand on Michael's thigh or knee, I couldn't see exactly which. "What are you reading, Michael?"

"Still *Desolation Angels.* Kerouac."

Kirby turned back to me and smiled. "We should go for a walk sometime, Colt. Especially since I can't drag this guy away from his books." She patted Michael's leg as she said it. I wondered how long they'd been together. Not long, I thought. Julia or Syd would've mentioned it.

"Colt likes it down at the bridge, too," Michael drawled. It was the first time he'd hinted about Julia and me, and I wondered why he was doing it. Did he want Kirby to find out? What for?

She smiled and raised her eyebrows at him, as if waiting for him to explain. I wondered what I had expected from Michael anyway. I stood up then and said, "I have to go. See you."

Dear C.M.,

I think I asked too much about your family tonight. Is that why you got so quiet? The thing is, I want to know what the rest of your life is like, not just the time we spend together.

That probably doesn't sound fair. I know we're only supposed to be having fun. I said so myself. But the truth is, you're more than that to me. And I think I'm more to you, even though you never say it.

What happens between us is amazing. It's not just the sex. Sometimes I wonder: If we came out from under the bridge and tried to be together all the time, would it still be this good, or would the whole thing fall apart?

It probably doesn't matter, because we're not going to come out from under the bridge. But I want to know you inside out.

∎ *chapter 9* ∎

My brother, Tom, came home for Thanksgiving, the first time we'd seen him since school started. He made his usual Tom kind of entrance, late Wednesday night. Dad was watching TV in the living room. Mom and I were in the kitchen, both with our feet up, thanks to long shifts at Barney's. It was the first shift I'd ever worked with her, and it would be the last if I had anything to say about it. I didn't need *two* bosses at the restaurant.

Tom flung open the front door and announced, "I have returned!"

"Hell yes you have!" Dad yelled, and gave him a big hug. Mom jumped up and ran into the living room. I stayed put. I figured Tom would find me as soon as he'd peeled our parents off of him.

He finally made it through the kitchen door. Mom trailed right behind him, saying, "I've got some roast beef in the fridge, if Colt didn't eat it all . . . and some ham . . ."

"No, I ate the ham," I said.

Tom whacked me on the shoulder. "Hey, stranger!"

"Hey, Tom."

"I can make you a sandwich," Mom said.

"Sit down," Tom told her. "I know how to work the refrigerator if I get hungry." He sat across the table from me. "So, Colt, I hear you're discovering the joys of minimum wage."

"Yeah, it's a thrill. . . . How's school?"

He launched into a story about his roommate making a mobile out of empty beer cans, and another about how he'd talked his math professor into giving him extra credit for writing an essay called, "Why Do We Need Math?" Those were only warm-ups for the full saga of Tom Goes to College. Nobody else said anything for a good hour or two, but I didn't mind. When he was on a roll, Tom was better than TV.

In the back of my mind, I was thinking that I might tell him about Julia this weekend. I was starting to feel like I would explode if I didn't talk to someone about it, and I could trust Tom. He might even have something useful to say. He had such an off-the-wall way of looking at things, he could come up with ideas that would never occur to me.

The whole family stayed up until midnight, listening to Tom, and then Dad set the alarm for five A.M. so he could put the turkey in the oven. Turkey was the one thing my father knew how to cook. He made it every year no matter how hungover he was, and he spent the whole day fussing over the stuffing and the basting. Once the bird was carved, his job for the year was done.

Tom grabbed the back of my shirt as we walked down the hall toward our rooms. "How are things around here lately?" he asked in a low voice. "They in a good mood?"

"Pretty good. Why?" I was about an inch taller than Tom now. It felt strange, not having to look up at him.

"I have some news for tomorrow." His eyes glinted. Knowing him, the news could be anything. He was going to ride on a space shuttle . . . he was fathering triplets . . . he'd decided to leave school and live naked in the desert . . . anything.

"Good or bad?"

"Oh, good, definitely good." Turning toward his room, he said, "At least, *I* think so."

Dear C.M.,
    Just had a Family Dinner, like Mom insists on having at least once a week. She's ecstatic when we're all home at the same time. I think it lives up to some fantasy about Happy Homes: candles in Ye Olde Family Candlesticks and smiling people chatting about their day.
    She gushed about Austin over dinner— she says he's so polite. She doesn't know he drinks himself blind. I love my mother but she's so naive sometimes!
    I'm trying to picture you having dinner with your family, but I can't. You don't

*talk much about them. I know who your
brother is—everybody knows your brother.
I can't imagine your parents, though. There
are too many blanks.*

Thanksgiving morning I went for a walk along the river. Then I took down the orange cone, and Tom and I shot targets in the backyard. He waited until we were all sitting around the table and had spent the usual five solid minutes praising Dad's turkey before he made his announcement.

"Because it's Thanksgiving," Tom said, spreading his arms wide, "and because I'm grateful to have such a wonderful family, who has always accepted me as I am, I wanted to share with you, on this special occasion, things I've learned about who I am."

"What?" Dad said. His mind was still on the turkey, but I don't think he could've followed that speech even if he'd been paying attention. It was pretty convoluted, even for Tom. I thought I knew what Tom was getting at, but I wasn't sure.

"Don't tell us you're joining a cult." Mom dumped a load of mashed potatoes onto his plate.

Tom laughed. "Not at all, not at all." Beaming, he said, "I just wanted you to know that I am gay."

Yes, I had guessed right. Mom and Dad froze, staring at him. I helped myself to the green beans.

"Now, there's nobody special in my life right now, but I wanted this out in the open, you know, in the interests of family communication."

"What the hell is this?" Dad growled. "Some kind of experiment?"

Tom's smile had begun to twitch. "Uh, no, of course not. Fact is, I've always been gay. I just didn't feel comfortable admitting it until recently."

When I thought about it, I realized that Tom had never had a girlfriend. Not that I'd bothered to think about it until just now, when he started babbling about knowing who he was. He'd gone out with girls once in a while, but usually in situations where he had to have a date, like proms or parties where all his friends had dates. He'd kissed Corrie Smith in the tree house, but he hadn't exactly raved about that experience. Well, now I knew why.

My parents stared at him while their dinner cooled. It was the first time I'd ever seen my mother fumble for words. "Tom," she finally said, "if this is one of your jokes—"

"It's not a joke."

"Son of a bitch," Dad said. He stood up and walked in a little circle behind his seat.

"I didn't think it would be such a shock." Tom glanced over at me. "Colt, *you* don't seem surprised."

"Not much." I looked at my father. "Come on, Dad, sit down."

"Tommy," Mom said, "are you sure?"

His smile faded. "Yes, Mom," he said quietly. "I'm sure."

"But—hell, you're so young, and you're always trying crazy new things—" She noticed me then, and slapped the fork out of my hand. "How can you eat?"

"It's dinnertime, that's how." I bent under the table to get my fork. "You know, he's not dying or anything."

"Tommy, don't you want to get married? Have kids?"

"I'd love to have kids someday. That's not out of the question."

"I need a drink," Dad said. He went over to the refrigerator. I hoped he wouldn't notice that Nick had snuck a couple of his beers yesterday.

"You don't need a drink," Mom said.

"Oh yes I do. I most certainly do." He snapped open a beer. "Christ. My own son—" He gagged. "You know what those guys do to each other?"

"Dad, I'm one of 'those guys.' And this is about more than just sex. It's about compatibility and love and—"

"You shut your fucking mouth." My father pointed the beer at him. "I don't want to hear that shit."

Tom looked at Mom. "What about you? How do you feel about this?"

"I'd like to know why the hell you sprang this at Thanksgiving dinner," she said. Behind her, Dad gulped his beer.

"Is it that big a deal? Is it so hard to accept?" He turned to me. "Colt. What about you?"

I struggled to swallow a mouthful of stuffing. "What?"

"I'm still your brother, right?"

"Sure."

"Who cares what that little snot thinks," Dad jumped in. "He's not paying your college bills. It's not his name you're dragging through shit."

My name was the same as theirs, of course, but logic was never one of my father's strengths.

"'Through shit?'" Tom said. "That's a little strong, don't you think?"

"I'm this close to kicking your ass. Don't push me."

"Dinner *and* a show," I mumbled. I only meant for Tom to hear, but my mother turned on me.

"We don't need your mouth right now, Mr. Smart-ass," she said.

I considered saying, "Let me know when you do," but decided to take more cranberry sauce instead.

"You are not my son anymore," Dad told Tom.

"Dad, hey, just give me a—"

"All right, enough," Mom cut in. She stood. "I'm going to lie down for a while. If I hear a sound from *any* of you before my head stops pounding, I'll kick some ass myself."

She went down the hall. Dad guzzled the rest of his beer, threw the can at Tom, and reached into the refrigerator for another.

"Dad," Tom said.

"Don't," Dad said, opening the beer. Then he took it out onto the back porch.

Tom sat there and watched me eat for a minute. I looked up and said, "Well, that went great." And then we both started to laugh. I hadn't laughed that hard in months. "This'll be a Thanksgiving to remember."

"Stop," he choked. When we finally stopped laughing, he began to eat. We both had as much as we wanted, but every now and then we had to stop and laugh again.

After dinner, Tom and I stuck the leftovers in the refrigerator and sat out on the back-porch steps. My father had gone around front to look at his wrecks, which is what he did whenever he wanted to feel better. I guess the cars were for him what the river was for me.

"So you're okay with this?" Tom asked me.

"Why should I care who you sleep with?" I didn't see how he could want to have sex with another guy, but hey, it was his life.

Tom looked out over the backyard, at the bleached weeds and the bare trees, the targets and the two dead cars. "You think he meant it when he said I'm not his son?"

"Nah, he was just being an asshole."

"I don't know." Tom pulled at his lower lip.

"Who cares, anyway? What do you think he's gonna do, make you turn in your royal title and your share of Windsor Castle?"

Tom rubbed the rough wood of the steps. "He mentioned the college money. You think he'll cut me off?"

"You're already paying for most of it, aren't you?" Tom had scraped up his tuition from scholarships and loans and a job at school.

"Yeah, but they're paying my living expenses. I suppose I could take out more loans if I had to." He shook his head. "I honestly thought it would go better than this. It's not like I ever pretended—well, I never had girls crawling all over my room."

"No, but you went out with them."

"All my friends were into girls. I kept waiting to feel the same way. I thought I'd wake up one day—" He took a breath. "Then I realized it was never going to happen. I liked guys, and that's the way I was going to stay." He frowned. "I hoped Mom and Dad would catch on without me having to make a big announcement."

"Who are you kidding?" I said. "You love big announcements."

He grinned. "Maybe. But I thought they'd figure it out when you started seeing Jackie. The rest of us kept falling over you two making out in every room of the house. I was sure they'd ask themselves, 'Hey, why doesn't Tom have a girl over? Why isn't Tom swapping spit with his girlfriend on the living-room couch?' But I guess people see what they want to see. At least you noticed something, didn't you?"

I shrugged. "Maybe. I never thought about it, but it didn't shock me or anything. It's like I knew it without thinking about it." I pointed to his twelve-foot wooden tower in the backyard. "Now I have new insight into your sculpture, though."

"What do you mean?"

"Well, we learned about phallic symbols in psych class—"

He laughed. "The symbolism wasn't intentional, believe me."

Mom opened the door then. "Colt, Syd's on the phone for you."

"Okay, thanks." I went inside and found my parents picking through the leftovers. Apparently they'd gotten their appetites back. My dad scowled at a bowl of squash, but it was my mother's face I watched. When Dad got upset, he would sulk on the sofa or drink until he passed out. Mom was the one who flared up and sometimes gave a whack or two to whoever was nearest. She also cooled down faster than he did, though. He could hold a grudge for years. I left plenty of room between them and me as I passed through the kitchen to my room.

I told Syd about our Thanksgiving to Remember, and she told me about her split holiday (morning with her mom, afternoon with her dad). "Should I come over tomorrow?" she said. "I can't wait to see you."

"I don't know. This is the first time I've seen my brother in a couple of months."

"Tommy won't mind. He knows me."

"I don't know, Syd."

"Don't you want to see me?"

What could I say to that? "Sure. I have to work at four, though."

"I can come over at noon. How's that?"

"Okay," I said, trying not to sound like I was making an appointment to have my teeth drilled.

"See you then."

I hung up and threw myself on my bed. I'd judged Julia pretty harshly for always saying she was going to break up with Austin Chadwick and never doing it, but now I was starting to see that it wasn't so easy.

■ *chapter 10* ■

Syd, Tom, and I shot targets in the backyard when she came over the next day. After she left, while I was getting ready for work, Tom came into my room and said, "So, you're going out with her now?"

"Sort of."

He sat on my bed. "Well, don't sound so excited."

"I kind of got dragged into it." Then I told him about how Syd had reached out for me the day her parents broke up, how I hadn't wanted to pull away from her then.

"So you don't like her?"

"Not that way."

"You're not doing her any favors, you know."

"Probably not." I plowed through my closet, looking for the bottom half of my uniform.

"The longer you let this go on, the worse it's going to get."

"I guess so." For some reason I didn't want to face him, but I finally turned around. He gave me that wise-older-brother look that used to give me a pain in the ass. It didn't bother me as much today, maybe because I knew he was right.

"Believe me," he said, pointing his finger at me like a gun, "no good comes from lying about what you really want."

The restaurant was busier than I'd expected. Apparently people were sick of their leftovers already. Michael Vernon came in around eight. He had coffee and a doughnut and read a book while he ate. "Where's Kirby?" I asked him.

"At her grandmother's," he said, without looking up.

"How'd you get here, anyway?" I was pretty sure he couldn't drive yet.

"Rode my bike." He turned a page, still without lifting his head. I left him alone after that. I could never quite figure him out. Sometimes he talked to me like a normal person, and other times he acted as if every word out of his mouth would cost him a pint of blood. I used to think maybe he was just uncomfortable with me because he knew about Julia, but I'd seen him treat Kirby the same way at school. It was as if he had an invisible igloo to retreat into whenever he felt like it.

"Smile, Colten!" Al the manager said as he policed the dining room. He'd recently come up with a truly sickening slogan, "Smiles sell steaks," which made me want to dump a tub of ranch dressing over his head. I turned my back to him, so he couldn't see whether I was smiling or not, and dragged a wet rag over a table.

What did I have to smile about? I was trapped in a bad situation with Syd, and my back and legs ached as if I were seventy instead of seventeen. When I got home tonight, my parents and brother would circle one another like Rottweilers in the local park, testing to see who would be the first to give ground. And worst of all, Julia was dead.

Julia had no patience with me when I got into a mood like this. "Don't sulk," she'd say, jabbing me in the ribs. "I'm the one who gets to be temperamental. I'm the spoiled rich one, remember?" If she couldn't make me laugh, she'd bait me until I flared up at her. She liked to set me off because, she said, it was so hard to do. "I love a challenge. Honestly, Colt, you have to be the calmest person alive." I swear if she could talk to me right now, she'd say something like, "Hey, stop acting like you're the one who's suffering. I'm the one who got killed, remember?"

When I got home with my head still full of Julia, a message was waiting for me: Syd had called. I didn't call her right back. I opened the notebook instead.

> Dear C.M.,
>   I want to break up with Austin, but we've got this wedding coming up at the end of December, a friend of both of our families. It would be awkward to break up before that. I know that sounds like a lame excuse, and maybe it is. But my life is so wrapped up with Austin's. Our families

know each other. We're always seeing
each other at picnics and dances and the
country club. We're in the same group of
friends. It's hard to get away from him.
Well, I don't expect you to understand.

I'm so confused. I think I like you
more than Austin, but you're so different,
your life is so different. And it's not easy
to break up with someone you've known for
such a long time.

Saturday night, I was on my bed with Syd, half our clothes off. She had come over, and again I'd let things go way too far. We hadn't had sex yet, but I got the feeling she wouldn't stop me if I tried. "I don't know what I'd do without you," she whispered.

"You'd survive just fine," I told her.

She gave a sort of shocked laugh and slapped my arm. "Colt! I mean it. You're the best thing in my life right now."

That did it. Tom was right; I wasn't doing her any good. I sat up and said, "No, I'm not."

"Yes, you—"

"Syd, look. I never should've started with you, because—" I choked on the words. I didn't want to hurt her, I really didn't. "I want to go back to being friends, the way we were before."

She sat up, too, her eyes wide. She wore a front-hook bra, which I had opened, but now she pulled it together in the middle. "Why?"

"It's the way I've felt all along. I just didn't have the nerve to tell you. Because of your parents . . ."

"So, what, you feel sorry for me? Screw that." She hooked her bra and yanked her shirt over her head. "Don't do me any favors."

"I know. I should've—well, I'm sorry."

"Where are my shoes?" She paced the floor, hunting for them. She picked up my shirt and threw it at me. I stayed on the bed, watching her, trying to find the right words so she would calm down and not hate me.

She knelt to peer under the bed. Then she looked up at me and said, "We're good together. Why do you want to wreck everything?"

I licked my lips, trying to figure out how much to tell her. "The truth is—there's somebody else."

"What?"

I didn't want to say it again.

"You've been seeing somebody behind my back?" she said.

"No. I mean there was somebody before you, and I'm not over it yet." I thought: *She's dead, but we won't go into that.*

"Jackie? You're still hung up on Jackie?"

"No, not Jackie."

She knelt there, staring at me. I noticed then that her T-shirt was on backward, the tag poking out of the neck hole. "You haven't had a girl since Jackie. How could you fall in love with someone and not tell me?"

"I didn't tell anybody." I reached over to touch the tag, to let her know her shirt was backward, but she jerked away.

"Who is it?" she asked.

"I can't tell you. Anyway, it's over now."

"You're unbelievable." She dragged a shoe out from beneath the bed. "You're such a liar! You made me think you loved me."

"I never said that."

"No, you just *acted* like it and let me *believe* it."

"I'm screwed up right now."

"You sure are." Her eyes brimmed over. "I don't want to see you, or talk to you, ever again." She found her other shoe and jammed her foot into it. Her jacket was stuck between the end of my mattress and the footboard. She wrenched at it, and I got up to help her.

I pulled the jacket free. "I know you're mad right now, but—"

"Go to hell." She grabbed the jacket and slammed out of my room. I flopped down on the bed and stuck the pillow over my head. I had done what I needed to do, but it didn't make things any better.

I had another dream about Julia that night. She came into Barney's with Austin when I was working, and I had to set a table for them and pretend I didn't know her. I tried to catch her eye, but she kept looking at Austin.

Then the scene switched, the way it does in dreams, and I was alone in the tree house with Julia. "I heard you're seeing somebody else now," she said.

"I was, but I had to break up with her."

"Because of me?"

"Partly, yes."

She smiled. Then her smile faded and she said, "I don't feel right. I think there's something wrong. . . ." She lifted her hand, and it was full of blood. Blood pooled in the palm of her hand and dripped all over the floor of the tree house, but I couldn't see where it was coming from.

"What happened?" I said. I grabbed her other hand, but that was bloody, too.

"I think it's from the accident," she said, frowning.

"What accident?"

"The *car* accident. It was very bad. Didn't you hear about it?"

I woke up then.

chapter 11

On Sunday Tom went back to school and I went walking down by the river, alone. When I got to the bridge, I crossed under it to the south side. The bank was rockier here; boulders jutted into the water.

I passed some small ripples that barely counted as rapids. The Willis River was no whitewater paradise. I looked around, remembering that Kirby had said that she came here sometimes, but I didn't see her today. Or anyone else.

I sat on a log and watched the water. I had seen the river just about every way you could. Chocolate-colored after floods, green and still in August, boiling during storms, hard-skinned in January. Today it ran blue and serious, a real winter river.

I knew that if I stuck my hand in, the water would burn and sting and turn my skin red. When we were little, Nick and Paul and I would dare each other. We'd grit our teeth and plunge our hands in, count to three, pull them out and howl. Then we'd stick them in our armpits, to ward off frostbite.

I had to laugh, remembering that. And still I felt the smallest itch to do it again today, to walk up to that water and let it sear my hand, shock me all the way through.

When Nick picked me up for school that week, I had the whole back-seat to myself, since Syd and Fred weren't there. "The lovebirds want to be alone," Paul smirked.

"What lovebirds?"

"Syd and Fred."

"Syd and Fred?" I asked, not sure I'd heard right.

"Yeah, he's been slobbering over her for two months," Nick said.

Paul laughed. "You shouldn't have let her go, Colt, because he snagged her like *that*." He snapped his fingers.

"I don't own her," I said. "She can go out with anybody she wants."

"That's the truth." They kept laughing.

I had a hard time believing that Syd liked Fred, especially this soon. But it was none of my business. I'd messed up things enough with her as it was.

Tom called that week, while I lay on my bed recovering from a shift at Barney's and thinking up excuses not to start studying for finals. "Hey, could you send me my walking stick?" he asked.

"Your what?"

"You know, Grandpa's old walking stick. I think it's in my closet somewhere. A friend of mine wants to use it in a play."

"How the hell would I mail it?"

"Well, could you at least look for it? Just let me know if it's there."

"All right."

He sighed. "So, have Mom and Dad come around yet?"

"Oh, you know Mom. She's okay. I don't know about Dad. He still won't mention your name."

"That'll change," he said, but he sounded like he was trying to convince himself.

"It will. Don't worry about it."

"Thanks, mate."

Mate. He must've been watching some Australian movie; I could even detect that Down Under accent creeping into his voice. The last time he saw an English movie, he called me "old chap" for three days. My brother loved to experiment—with accents, clothes, hobbies, whatever. No wonder my parents thought being gay was something he might just be trying out for a while.

At work Al made me put up decorations. I don't know why he picked me, since I was probably the least festive person who worked there. And to make the job even less fun, he hovered, criticizing my wreath-hanging technique. "Don't just plunk it on the nail like that," he said. "Try to look happy, can't you?"

"You mean, show some holiday spirit?" He'd told me approximately forty-five times that afternoon to "show some holiday spirit."

"Exactly."

While I wound silver garlands around everything that would hold them, I thought about the Christmas before, and Julia. I was stuck on an entry in her notebook from last December. I had read past it and on into January. But then I'd gone back to it, reading it over and over until now I couldn't get the words out of my head if I tried.

> Dear C.M.,
> I love Christmas. I feel like a little kid again. I love all the corny songs and TV shows. I love the lights and decorations, the red and gold and glitter. I've always hated it when they tear everything down in January, when everything goes gray and white again. Blech.
> Michael and I used to hunt all over the house for our presents. I got so psyched to find them, especially the things I really wanted and wasn't sure I was going to get. Like this pink stuffed horse one year—don't ask me why it had to be pink!
> I want to get you something, but I don't know what. Anything we give each other, we'll have to explain to people. But I'll come up with an idea.

She'd ended up giving me a book, Jon Krakauer's *Into the Wild*. It was a good choice. I'd wanted to read it, and she knew that a book was something I could just stick on my shelf without anyone noticing it or asking who had given it to me.

But I hadn't gotten her anything.

"I didn't know we were giving presents," I said, while we huddled in the back of her car, under a blanket she'd brought.

"That's okay," she said, in this tone that told me it was definitely not okay.

I didn't know, I wanted to say again. And I couldn't even explain why I didn't know, why it hadn't occurred to me to get her a gift, why I hadn't realized she might give me one. I guess I thought of all that as real-world, girlfriend-boyfriend stuff, something she shared with Austin but not with me. For the most part, Julia and I made up the rules of our relationship without talking about them; we both seemed to just know them. Not this time.

I didn't know how to fix it, either, because anything I got her now would seem forced. "I'm sorry," I said.

She turned and looked me in the eyes as best she could in the dimness. The streetlight on the bridge gave us no true colors; she was silver and black. I felt the heat of her under the blanket. I wasn't sure whether the space between us had been warmed by her or me or both of us; I couldn't tell where the dividing line was.

"It doesn't matter," she said, and the thing was, I could tell she meant it. She let it go. Even in her notebook, in the entries after that night, she didn't mention it. It was something she could've held against me but didn't.

The week before Christmas, this first Christmas without Julia, we got eight inches of snow. I went out and shoveled it off the driveway. The sun was setting as I finished, streaking the sky with purple. The snow muffled everything. All I could hear was the scrape of my shovel. The bushes looked like they'd been dipped in cream frosting. It was so good to be outside that I didn't even mind the shoveling.

Kirby Matthews came walking down the plowed street. I stopped shoveling when I saw her. Her hair was black and her coat was black, so she stood out against all that white.

"Colt," she said. "Out playing in the snow?"

"If you want to call it that." I hefted the shovel.

"Don't you have a snowblower?"

"My father broke it last winter." He'd actually rammed it into the side of the house while drunk, but I didn't feel like sharing that particular family story with her. "What are you doing all the way down here?"

"Walking." She came to stand near me, out of the road. "I like to walk in the snow."

"And Michael doesn't, I guess."

"Not really." She wrinkled her nose. "He'd rather be inside. But I'd suffocate if I was in the house all day."

"Me, too."

"We watched a whole marathon of movies today—you know, the old black-and-white kind where everyone smokes and they're all wearing hats, and every time something dramatic happens, the background music goes crazy?"

"Yeah."

"We love those movies. Michael has half the lines memorized. But after a while, I just had to get outside."

We stood there looking at each other. Then she said, "Sorry about you and Syd."

"Oh . . ." I didn't know what to say about that. "Thanks."

We got quiet again. For some reason, these silences weren't awkward. Maybe it was the snow lying everywhere, making stillness seem okay. Then she said, "You going out somewhere?"

"No, why?"

"You're shoveling out the car."

"Oh—no, my mother's working tonight. I told her I'd get the car out for her. But I don't work until tomorrow."

"Where?"

"Barney's Steakhouse."

"I know that place. . . . My parents took us when we were little. I used to love it." She laughed. "Does it still have the crayons and the kiddie place mats to draw on?"

"Yeah. Only the kids draw on everything else, too."

She laughed again. "Well, I'd better get going. It's getting dark."

"I could drive you. I'm almost done here."

"What about your mother?"

"I'll be back before she has to go."

"Oh. Well, okay."

She stood there while I finished. I told her she should go in the house, but she said she wasn't cold. She liked looking at the world while the snow was still fresh, she said.

Mom was glad to let me warm up the car for her, so I took Kirby home. We didn't talk on the ride to her house, but again that was okay. I was very aware of her in the seat next to me. I almost thought I could hear her breathing, even over the grinding *chug* of the engine and the rasping of the tires on the plowed roads.

"Thanks, Colt," she said as she got out of the car.

"Anytime." I was sort of wishing it had been a longer drive. Kirby was the first person I'd been with in a while who made me feel relaxed.

◼ chapter 12 ◼

Dear C.M.,

    I couldn't see you last Friday because
Pam needed to talk to me. She's my best
friend, so I knew you would understand.

    Pam's always telling me I should break
up with Austin. She thinks he doesn't
treat me very well, and I guess sometimes
he doesn't. I don't mean he hits me or
anything. But he takes me for granted.
He's not too interested in what's going on in
my head. He likes me to be around, to listen
to him, to dance with him. Sometimes Pam
and I joke that we could make a Julia
doll and send it on dates with him. Austin
would never know the difference.

Yeah, right. There were pages of entries like this in Julia's note-book. And still she'd stayed with Austin.

Tom came home for Christmas, but Dad still wasn't speaking to him. Once or twice Dad sort of grunted at him, which Tom said was the first crack in the dam. My brother always was an optimist. Mom was better than Dad—she mostly treated Tom normally—but she some-times got this uncomfortable look on her face, as if my brother had grown a long scaly tail or a second head and she was trying not to stare at it. I dealt with the whole thing by working almost every day over the break.

One night Kirby came into Barney's with Pam Henderson. I hadn't seen Pam in months. She'd been away at boarding school, but I guessed she was home for vacation. It took me a minute to rec-ognize her. She'd gotten thin and quiet, and her hair hung down in dull strings. Before, she'd been one of those sickeningly perky girls who never shut up. She and Julia were always giggling over their own private jokes. And now she was the first person I'd seen who showed Julia's death on her face.

Kirby smiled and said, "Which section is yours, Colt?"

"This side of the room. I'm busing, though—I'm not a waiter."

"That's okay. Pam, why don't you get that table for us?" To me Kirby murmured, "She doesn't want to see any of the Black Moun-tain kids, so I thought I'd bring her here."

"Yeah, they don't usually pollute themselves by crossing Barney's threshold, that's for sure," I said.

"I'm sorry, Colt, I didn't mean it that way."

"Forget it."

They ordered coffee and pie. It was about ten thirty and pretty slow, so the manager gave me a break. Kirby asked me to sit down with them.

Pam ate her pie without looking at me. I couldn't stop staring at her, though. She'd been the last person to see Julia alive. She knew what had happened that night. "How are you doing, Pam?" I asked.

"Okay," she said, still focused on her plate.

"How do you like your new school?" God, I sounded like a long-lost uncle at her family reunion. But I didn't know what else to say, how to start.

"It's okay."

I wished she would at least look at me. Maybe I could read something in her eyes. The weird thing about seeing Pam after so long was that it made me feel like Julia could come back, too, as if Pam were a gateway to Julia. Time folded back to the night of the accident. I heard the rain hit my bedroom windows again, remembered Syd's call. That night I'd still had clothes in my room that smelled of Julia. I'd kept them out of the wash for a few weeks, but her scent had faded anyway.

"Do you still see Austin and those guys?" I asked now, just for something to say.

"No." Pam stabbed a gooey chunk of apple, stuck it into her mouth, and chewed.

Obviously she wasn't going to volunteer anything. Why should she? I had to push a little. "I guess you miss Julia."

"Yes."

Kirby gave me a warning look. I knew I should shut up, but somehow I couldn't. I had to know what had happened. Every detail.

"Why did she get drunk that night? She didn't usually."

"I don't want to talk about it," Pam said. She chopped a chunk of pie crust into halves, quarters, and then it crumbled. "Besides, how do you know what she 'usually' did? You didn't know her."

I watched Kirby's fork sink into a piece of pie. I told myself to stop here, to let that night alone. But Pam was the only person who could tell me what I wanted to know. My stomach clenched. "Did she pass out in the car?" I said. "Was she unconscious when the car hit— what did it hit, anyway?" Kirby kicked me under the table.

"I said I don't want to talk about it." Pam pushed her plate away. "God. You didn't even know her."

"I know," I said, my stomach lurching. A hot wave washed over me, and I swallowed. Somehow I thought everything would be okay if I could be sure that Julia had felt no pain. "But I need to— Look, if she passed out, and didn't know what hit her, that's better than if—"

Pam shoved back her chair and ran out of there. Kirby said, "What is *wrong* with you, Colt?"

"I'm sorry."

She stared at me as if I'd butchered a few puppies in front of her. "What the hell *was* that?" She dug in her pocket for money.

"Don't," I said. "I'll take care of the check."

"Yeah, I guess it's the least you can do." She gave me another disgusted glare and left the restaurant.

I cleared the table and walked over to the register to pay the bill. Then I went into the men's room and threw up.

Sunil, one of the waiters, was standing at the sinks when I came out of the stall. "Are you sick?" he asked.

I rinsed out my mouth at the sink. "Yeah. No. I'll be okay."

"You should go home."

"I'm off in an hour anyway. Don't worry about it."

I went back to clearing tables. My hands shook a little, but I didn't think anyone could tell. As long as I didn't drop anything, who would care?

I drove home on autopilot. I was standing in the kitchen pouring out antacids from one of the industrial-size bottles my father always bought, when Tom came in. "Did you have dinner at Barney's?" He laughed, nodding at the pills.

"Yeah, funny." I crunched down on a couple of the tablets. "Dad talking to you yet?"

"I got a couple more grunts out of him. I think he's coming around." Tom opened the refrigerator and stared into it. I had to turn away from the sight of the food.

I went to my room and opened the notebook, although part of me didn't even want to touch it. I had reached the first entry from March.

> Dear C.M.,
> I saw you talking to Lindsay Scanlon in the halls today. I see you with Syd all the time and that doesn't bother me—she's really like one of the guys, isn't she? But

for some reason I wanted to jab Lindsay
in the eyeballs. You don't have to tell me
that's not fair. I know it's not. And I still
want to know what you were talking about
with her!

Sometimes when I see you at school,
it's like you're not the same person I meet
down at the bridge. I look at you and think:
He was with me the other night, he told me
about a fight with his father, he wore his
big muddy boots in my car and I had to
hose off the floor mats the next morning, he
ran his tongue along my neck, he was inside
me. And it seems like I made the whole
thing up, because we don't talk in public,
and even the mud in my car doesn't seem
real. But you belong to me, in a strange way
that I can't explain.

chapter 13

At school Syd advertised her relationship with Fred.
She was always touching him, ruffling his hair, rubbing his back. I
felt like it was a play she put on, and I didn't want to watch. That first
day back from vacation, I left our lunch table as soon as I was done
eating and decided to finish the break in the library.

Kirby caught up with me as I left the cafeteria. "Hey," she said.
"Can I talk to you a minute?"

"Okay." I figured if she wanted to yell at me again about that night
at Barney's, I deserved it. She didn't look mad, but maybe she was
saving it up until we were alone.

She pulled me into an empty classroom and closed the door. It
was so quiet that I heard the hand on the wall clock click forward.

"I know about you and Julia," she said.

Had she guessed or did she really know? I wished more than ever
that I'd kept my stupid mouth shut at Barney's. I thought about

denying it, but I was sick of lying. I'd spent hours of Christmas vacation gorging on Julia's notebook, reliving last spring and summer, smelling the river mud and her peach shampoo all over again.

"Michael told me," Kirby went on. "I couldn't believe the things you said that night. . . . I wanted to strangle you. I was ranting about what a jerk you'd been, and he told me why you were so interested in what happened to Julia. Then at least it made sense."

I cleared my throat. "Does Pam know?"

"No. I think you should tell her, though."

She was right. But whenever I remembered the look on Pam's face while I'd tried to gouge the bloody details out of her, I wanted to puke again.

Kirby said, "Does anybody else know?"

"Just Michael."

She stared into my eyes, as if trying to read the imprint of Julia on my brain. "How long were you seeing her?"

"A year."

"Wow." She frowned. "You and Austin."

I sat down on one of the desks. "Yeah, me and Austin." It was strange to be connected with him that way.

She sat down, too. "How did you even manage it? She was always—oh. Forget that, I'm sorry. You don't have to tell me."

"We met late at night, down by the river."

She chewed her lip, thinking. "Michael said that Julia never knew what she wanted . . . that she didn't like to choose, she always wanted everything."

"That's a good way to put it."

"How are you doing, Colt?"

I shrugged and said, "Okay." Then I thought about that night at Barney's. "Most of the time."

"Well, I know what Pam and Michael have been through, and it's been awful."

"It's not easy, that's true." That was the most I would say. I wasn't going to slice myself open for her, spill juicy gore out onto the desktop.

She reached out and rested her fingers on my shoulder. Her hand slid an inch, then another, down my arm. It sent shock waves through me—something about being touched when she was so close to the truth, when I was admitting things I'd never told anyone. Her fingers seemed to burn off the layers of my skin, press into the nerves. I told myself I was just overreacting because no girl had touched me since Julia. And then I remembered that wasn't even true. I'd forgotten about Syd.

Kirby might have noticed I was holding my breath; she dropped her hand. "Well, I'm sorry, Colt. If you ever want to talk about it, you can talk to me. I won't tell anyone."

"Thanks." We sat there for a minute, staring at each other, the way we had the day of the snowstorm. Only this time, she knew everything. I wasn't sorry Michael had told her.

I had a shift at Barney's that afternoon, but while I was getting ready, my father barged into my room. Apparently he had remembered that I lived there.

"Come outside and look at the cars," he said.

"I can't. I'm busy."

"It'll only take a minute."

"Dad, come on," I groaned. "I have to go to work."

"Just for a minute."

I finally agreed to tour the front yard when it was clear he wouldn't leave me alone otherwise. He always believed that if he stood me in front of the cars long enough, talking up their potential, I would fall in love. Never mind that this had failed every other time he'd tried it.

While he poured out his usual sales pitch, I snuck looks at my watch. I broke into his speech to point at one of the wrecks. "Dad, you had mice nesting in that thing, and there's a tree growing out of the back. You think you'll ever get it running?"

He slammed his mouth shut, whirled around, and stalked back into the house. I hadn't expected him to get that upset. Tom and I used to tease him about the cars all the time. I almost went into the house after him, but I was late for my shift.

Dad didn't say a word to me that night, but that wasn't unusual. Most times, if he had his beer and his TV, he didn't want to talk to anybody. What did surprise me was that on Saturday he had all the wrecks hauled away.

I came home from work to an empty yard. At first, I thought he must've moved the cars to the backyard—maybe because of the annual nagging from the neighbors—until I discovered that the two in back were also gone. I went into the house and found my father sitting in front of the TV with a beer. "What happened to all the cars?"

"What do you care?" he growled at the screen.

"I was just wondering."

"I got sick of looking at them."

I didn't believe that, but he obviously wasn't going to tell me, so I went into the kitchen. My mother was soaking her feet and having a beer while she watched something boil on the stove. "How was your shift?" she asked.

"Okay. Where are the cars?"

She grunted. "He's still pissed about Tommy. He's been rambling on about how you're the only son he's got left, how he wants to work on the cars with you. I told him if he's going to try this male bonding shit, he should take you fishing or hunting. Bring home something we could eat." She picked up her beer and went on, "When you didn't give a crap about the cars, he gave up on the whole thing. At least this summer we'll be able to mow the front lawn again."

"I get it," I said, and sat down across from her. "We're not the sons he wanted."

"Oh, don't be so dramatic. Your brother gives us enough of that." She sipped her beer and sucked foam off her top lip. "What's going on with you nowadays? You flunking out of school? How are your grades?"

"Okay. The usual."

"Oh yeah? Got any girlfriends? Boyfriends?"

I laughed. She put her beer down. I could see all the little veins and red spots and wrinkles in her skin. I wondered if it was her job that made her look so much older than she was. I could see how it would; Barney's was aging me, too. Nothing in my life had made me want to go to college as badly as this job did.

"Mom, I'm not gay." I rolled her beer can between my hands,

feeling the liquid slosh inside. "And it's not the worst thing in the world that Tom is, right?"

"Colt, maybe someday you'll understand what it's like to think you know a person and then find out different." She snatched the beer back.

I took a shower and went to my room. I got into bed with the purple notebook, looking to forget about Barney's and my family.

> Dear C.M.,
>   I couldn't stop laughing last night. I've never seen you laugh so hard either. I guess we were both in a weird mood!
>   I've never had that much fun with Austin. Which makes me wonder, seriously, what am I doing with him? We've outgrown whatever we had.

I sighed. The last thing I wanted to read was another entry about Austin Chadwick. As for the night Julia was talking about, a night last August, I did remember us getting on one of those laughing jags where everything seems funny. We hadn't been high or anything, except maybe on each other. I couldn't remember the exact jokes we'd made—something about frogs, or crickets? It probably wouldn't seem funny now. You had to be there.

I didn't want to finish reading. What was I going to find, more excuses about why she had to stay with Austin?

There was another reason I didn't want to keep reading. I fingered the remaining pages with her writing on them: only a few. It was January now but August in Julia's notebook, and I knew the end was coming. I didn't remember every detail about every moment with her, I didn't remember the frog jokes or whatever we'd laughed about last summer, but I remembered the last time I'd seen her. Now I would have to relive that night, and the way we'd ripped into each other, through her eyes. Then I would hit the blank pages, and it would be over.

▪ *chapter 14* ▪

I couldn't get Syd to talk to me. When we were all
in a group and she couldn't avoid it, she'd say a few words. Very few,
each one edged in ice. It wasn't what I would call talking, not like
before.

Even at lunch, she ignored me. Fred sat practically on top of her,
glaring at me if I moved too close. I wondered what she had told him
about our breakup to put that look on his face. Whatever it was, it
made our table as much fun as a minefield.

Kirby saw what was happening and probably heard about it from
Syd, too. She asked me to sit with her and Michael. The first time I
did it, Nick told me to watch my back. "You can't trust Black Mountain," he said.

"Kirby's not Black Mountain."

"Then why is she always with those guys? I'm telling you, look
out."

I liked sitting with Kirby because it was okay with her if I didn't say anything. Michael never felt obligated to open his mouth just because other people were with him, so sometimes the three of us ate in silence. Other times, Kirby and I talked about hiking along the river, while Michael read his books. Then there were the days I listened to them ramble on about their favorite old movies. They also got very excited about a college radio station—"the only one we get around here that doesn't play sugar-coated shit," in Michael's words. Some days I let them be alone together while I sat at my old table and put up with the freeze from Syd and Fred. I went back and forth, feeling like I didn't completely belong in either place.

One night at the end of January, Kirby came into Barney's alone. She said Michael was home studying for an exam. She ordered hot chocolate and talked to me while I finished my shift. Then we went outside together.

We didn't get into our cars right away; we stopped to stare at the icicles hanging from the roof of the restaurant. They ranged from huge pillars to little points; they grew on top of one another and fused into amazing shapes.

Our breath made clouds in the air, and my ears ached from the cold. Snow had fallen a few days earlier, and the leftovers had frozen into a couple of inches of dirty white grit. We stood at the edge of the parking lot, our feet crunching on the ground as we took small steps back and forth to keep warm.

"I got an e-mail from Pam," Kirby said. "I keep wanting to tell her about you and Julia. To explain why you acted the way you did at Christmas."

"Don't," I said. "I should do it myself."

"Do you want her address?"

I swallowed. "Okay. Yeah."

"I'll give it to you."

We stood there, the stars looking extra sharp and clear the way they usually do in winter, my toes going numb. Still I didn't want to leave.

"Did you hear about that kid from Deerhaven who fell into the river?" Kirby said.

I had. He'd fallen through thin ice several miles upriver of our town. He'd frozen to death before they even pulled him out of the water. "Yeah, what about him?"

"I don't know. I was thinking of him because I was down at the river yesterday, and I really wanted to go onto the ice."

"I'm glad you didn't."

"Yeah, well, I don't take chances like that." She sighed, and the steam from her breath rose and vanished. "It's freezing. I should get going."

"Me, too," I said.

Now she took a step away from me, toward her car. "Good night."

"Good night."

"Aren't you going?" She took another step.

"Yeah."

"You realize you're just standing there in one spot."

"Uh-huh."

She walked backward to her car, watching me. "Good night," she called again.

"See you." But I didn't move until after she'd driven off.

I went home and sat alone on my bed. My parents were asleep, and they'd turned the heat down. I sat there with my coat still on. I usually didn't mind being alone, but tonight I minded. I looked at the phone. Once I would've called Syd, but I couldn't do that now.

Shadows piled up in the corners of my room. I breathed in. The quiet made my ears feel hollow. I thought of Kirby standing with me in the parking lot, talking about thin ice. I thought of Julia standing with me on the riverbank last winter, daring me to walk across the frozen river. I hadn't done it. She'd taken a step onto the ice, and I'd pulled her back, and when she play-fought me, I carried her up to her car.

I looked over at my desk, at the purple notebook. I'd been waiting to finish it—waiting for what, I wasn't sure. Now I went over to the desk and opened it. Standing there, I read the final entries from August. I read her words about summer nights and mosquitoes and the slow black warmth of the river, about hot mist and the taste of salt on our skin. And then I sat on my bed and read the only entry from last September.

> Dear C.M.,
> Tonight I'm going to break up with Austin. I'll do it at Adam's party. I figure I can tell him and then he'll go off with his friends and get drunk, and I can hang out with Pam. What do you think? This secrecy thing is getting old, isn't it? It was exciting at first, but now I'm tired of sneaking

around. And maybe you are, too. Maybe that's why you acted the way you did the other night.

I know I've talked before about getting rid of Austin, but this time I mean it. I'm going to start my senior year with a clean slate. And you know what? I'm not doing it for you. After all, in spite of what you said on Friday, you seem fine with what we have now. I want to break up with Austin for myself, not because it's what you want but because it's what I want.

Wish me luck. It will be hard—I can't deny that. I've known him for so long. But it's not fair to him, all this lying, all this wishing I were someplace else. It's time to end it.

The next time I see you, I'll be free!

The notebook ended there.

Every time I'd opened it, I had thought the next page would be the one to tell me what I needed to know. Now I'd run out of pages.

More than anything else in the notebook, I had wanted to read this entry, the last one. I wanted to know what Julia thought about the last time we saw each other. I wanted to know if it ate away at her the way it did at me. But she hadn't said much about it after all.

Sometimes I wondered why she'd written this book. She'd never given it to me, or even told me about it. But then, the Colt she was writing to was not exactly me. She had told him a lot more than she'd told me. He was more dependable than I was; he didn't talk back or have moods of his own. He didn't pick a fight with her on the last night he'd ever seen her.

If she'd broken up with Austin, would she still have needed me? If she could see me or talk to me anytime, instead of squeezing our whole relationship into Friday nights and unsigned notes and secret phone calls, would she still have wanted me?

And would I have wanted her? At first, the whole thing seemed like such a great idea. Heaven had dropped right into my lap: sex with no strings attached. I should've known there are always strings. They'd slipped around my wrists and knotted up before I'd even noticed. They still pulled at me, still chafed.

Kirby gave me Pam's address, and I wrote Pam a letter. I didn't e-mail her, because I didn't want to make it easy for her to forward my message to sixty thousand people. Pam could tell half of Black Mountain that I was claiming to have slept with Julia Vernon, and they'd love to come after me for it. But even though it was a risk, I had to write her. Not only did I owe her an apology for the way I'd acted at Barney's, but I needed to know more about Julia's last night.

It took her two weeks, until the middle of February, to answer. I spent those two weeks working, going to school, scraping ice off the driveway, hanging out with Nick or Kirby but never with Syd, and rereading the notebook. I don't know what I thought I would see in Julia's words that I hadn't seen already.

I came home from an eight-hour Saturday shift to find Pam's letter on the kitchen table. I didn't open it right away. I took a shower, thinking about the letter the whole time. Then I took it into my room and looked at it, the way I'd looked at the purple notebook that first afternoon. I held it, weighed it in my hand. It was a thick letter, so I was pretty sure she hadn't written just to tell me to leave her alone.

Finally I opened it: fat loopy writing on little blue sheets of paper.

Colt: Thanks for your letter. At first I thought you had some nerve writing to me, but now I've read your letter a couple of times and I think I understand. Honestly, at first I thought you were playing a stupid joke on me, making up this whole story about you and Julia. Then I remembered this one time when we were at our lockers and she was complaining about Austin and I said something like, "Oh, but you know you love him," because she was always going on like that. And she smiled and said, "What if I told you I was in love with somebody else?" I jumped all over that, trying to find out what she meant, until she backed off and said it was only a joke. But there was another time when we bumped into you in the hall and she got all jittery and confused and you gave her this long look. I didn't think it meant anything then. At least now I get why you were such an asshole at Xmastime.

So you want me to tell you Julia passed out and never knew what hit her, right? Well, I can't tell you that. Maybe she did and maybe she didn't. I think she probably didn't. Because what happened was she got drunk, falling-on-the-floor drunk, and I put her in my car and she rolled down the window. She wouldn't fasten the seat belt because she said it made her sick to have anything around her waist. I put it on her even though she didn't want it. She might've unclicked it on the ride up, though.

She kept sticking her head out the window. Then she'd kind of loll back in the seat and mutter or laugh to herself. She was completely bombed. Maybe that's as good as being passed out, because she sure wasn't feeling any pain. Not then, anyway.

I don't remember the crash. We skidded on the wet road, I know that. I remember driving and then skidding with everything

whirling by the windows, and then I remember
being outside the car, wandering in the road,
wondering what happened. Looking at my
car all smashed up and screaming for Julia.
We had run into one of the stone posts at the
end of the Melvilles' driveway, but I don't
remember actually hitting it.

I stopped reading and closed my eyes. Well, this was what I had
asked for, all right. The details. I could see the stone post, all the stone
posts on Black Mountain Road. Why did they need those things at
the ends of their driveways, anyway? I opened my eyes and contin-
ued reading, not because I wanted to anymore, but because I had to.

I called 911 on my cell phone, but
somebody who'd heard the crash had already
done it. These people came out of their house
and put a blanket on me. When I tried to go
to the car they turned me around and walked
me the other way. My arm hurt and they
said it was probably broken, and my head
hurt, and there was no way I thought Julia
was dead. I was covered with that air-bag
powder, so I thought even if Julia had taken
off her seat belt the air bag would've saved
her. Since nobody would let me near the car,
I knew she was hurt pretty bad, but I never

in a million years guessed she was dead. In fact, it took me weeks to believe it.

I don't remember the exact crash, just before and after it. The doctor says it's common not to remember an accident. The trauma interrupts your brain from making memories. So the crash will always be a blank spot and I'm glad.

You asked what Julia was like at the party, if she was happy, why she got drunk. She told me she wanted to break up with Austin. She kept having another drink to give her courage, or maybe to get her to the point where she didn't care what she said. She drank so much so fast that Austin got disgusted with her and told me to take her home.

That was a real laugh, let me tell you. It was okay for HIM to get totally bombed whenever he wanted, but if he had to take care of her, forget it! She called him a hippocryte (is that how you spell it?) and a pompous ass, but he thought it was the booze talking. He laughed at her and waved good-bye while I dragged her out of there. She didn't get to break up with him the way she planned.

So Julia hadn't broken up with Austin. She hadn't tied that up, finished it off. I guess I always knew it. But here's the question: did she drink too much so she could break up with him, or did she drink too much so she wouldn't have to?

I'll tell you the truth, Colt, I wrote this letter not sure if I'd ever send it, thinking maybe I'd tear it up. But I'm actually kind of glad I wrote it. This is the first time I've talked about that night in detail, except to this counselor guy they made me see. I told him some things because I was supposed to, but really I didn't want to talk about it. Because the fact is, it's my fault. The hardest part ever was looking Julia's parents in the face afterward. Even though it was an accident, I was driving. Maybe if I'd driven slower or concentrated more or steered the car a little bit differently, she would be alive. How do you think I can live with that? You wrote that you feel guilty. That's funny, Colt, that's really funny because who are you to feel guilty? I'm the one.

I don't know exactly what you're looking for, but I've told you everything I know. I hope it helps. I know what it's like to keep thinking about Julia, to keep thinking what-if. Anyway I'm trying to get on with my life and just accept it because there's nothing I can do about the past. You just have to live with it.

—Pam

Tom had spring break at the beginning of March, when the trees were bare and the mud still had shards of ice in it. He came home for two days. He planned to spend the other seven in Florida, driving down with some guys from school. They were taking turns so they could drive straight through.

I was the only one home when he got there, since Mom was working at Barney's and Dad had a tiling job, for a change. I was lying on the rug watching TV when Tom burst in the front door. His entrance shook the living-room walls. "I didn't recognize the place," he said. "Without those junkers in front, the house looks almost respectable. If we chop down the trees growing out of the gutters, we might really have something."

"Well, feel free to start chopping. Before they get me to do it."

He flopped down on the couch. "Where're the parents?"

"Work."

"I notice you and Mom never work the same shifts."

"No, we'd drive each other crazy."

He stretched, then plunked his feet on the coffee table. "It's good to be home."

"Just don't make any big announcements this time, okay? They're still recovering from the last one."

He laughed. "I managed to control myself over Christmas, didn't I?"

"I guess."

"Oh, hey." He snapped his fingers. "Mom asked me to find out if you're on drugs."

"What?"

"You heard me."

"Why would she think that?"

"She says you've been very secretive this year." He laughed again. "I told her if you were really high all the time, you'd be a lot more cheerful."

"Mom's crazy."

"Well, we all know *that*, but . . . I told her it was highly ironic for her to worry about you taking drugs when Dad lies around here drinking seven days a week."

"You said that?"

"Yup. Since they're already pissed at me, I might as well say whatever's on my mind. It's actually quite liberating." He stood up. "Come on, my drug-addicted little brother, let's shoot some targets."

We went out back and shot for a while until Tom said, "You remember the old tree house?"

"Yeah."

"I wonder if it's still there."

"It is. I was up there last fall."

"Hey, let's go check it out."

"Nah, I don't think so." I never liked remembering the day I'd been there with Syd.

"Aw, come on." He hauled the orange cone up on the porch.

When we got to the side path that led to the tree house, though, I couldn't make myself go. "You go ahead," I told him. "I'm going down to the bridge."

So he went off in search of his childhood or whatever he was looking for, and I took the path that led to the bridge. I didn't make it that far, though. On the way, I ran into Kirby.

"I thought you liked the south side of the bridge better," I said.

"I do. That doesn't mean I stay there all the time."

"Well, welcome to the north side."

"Thanks."

We stood there looking at each other for a minute, in that way we had of not talking and not needing to talk. Her eyes were very dark. She swept a strand of long black hair behind her ear. "Where's Michael?" I said.

"Home, probably." She shrugged, keeping her eyes on mine. "We broke up last weekend."

"Oh. I didn't know that." I hadn't been in the cafeteria all week, which was where I usually saw Kirby and Michael. The weather had finally turned nice enough for me to eat outside. Hardly anyone else thought it was nice enough—I guess stray patches of snow and screaming March winds put them off. But I could feel spring coming, and I didn't mind eating alone.

"I'm sorry," I told Kirby. I had to force that a little bit. Michael was okay, but I'd always thought she could do better.

"That's all right. We're still friends."

Kirby and I began to walk together. We headed down toward the riverbank. "He's a good guy, you know?" she said, stopping to untangle her hair from a twig she'd snagged it on. "Just a little—intense."

We reached the water's edge. I thought she was going to say more about Michael, but instead she asked me, "Did you ever write to Pam?"

"Yeah." I bent down, picked up a handful of stones, and flung one into the river.

"Did she write back?" Kirby scooped up stones, too.

"Yes, she did."

Silence, except for the sound of our rocks plunking into the water. I knew she was waiting for me to tell her about Pam's letter. But keeping my mouth shut about Julia was too much of a habit by now. Finally Kirby said, "I hope she told you whatever you needed to know."

"I don't want to talk about it, if you don't mind."

"Okay." She threw her last stone. Then she turned to face me.

I had the feeling she was going to say she had to leave, and I didn't want her to go yet. "Come with me a minute," I said. I took a few steps backward, watching to see if she would follow. She did, raising her eyebrows as if to ask where we were going.

I led her along the riverbank to a spot where a feeder stream came in. It made a waterfall there: only a few feet high, but nice to look at. At least it was something to show her.

"I never knew this was here." She bent down to wet one hand.

"Ooh, it's cold. But doesn't it look like spring? The water and the rocks and the moss . . . it's so green." She looked up at me.

"Yes," I said, because she seemed to expect it. But I wasn't looking at the water. I was watching her, the curve of her mouth and the way she flicked droplets off her hand. A couple of the drops spattered my jeans.

"Thanks for showing me, Colt." She wiped her hand on her jacket and smiled at the waterfall.

For days after that, I thought about calling Kirby. I had nothing to say, but I kept wanting to talk to her anyway. It wasn't until Thursday that I understood why.

That night I had a dream about her, the kind of dream I used to have about Julia. The kind of dream that made me check the sheets in the morning. After that, it was pretty obvious to me what was going on. Any idiot would've figured it out sooner, but she was the first girl I'd liked since Julia, and I realized I'd been going around thinking I would never feel that way again. But now it was all rushing in on me in a hot flood, and I didn't want to think about anything else but Kirby.

I saw Michael on Friday. He came up to my locker before lunch. He was always pale, as if he spent most of his life locked in his basement, but today he looked even worse. Not only white, but wrung out, like he'd given double blood donations. "Eat with me," he said.

"I'm going outside."

"It's like a tornado out there."

"That's okay, I don't care."

His voice dropped. "I can't sit alone in that cafeteria while Kirby's in there."

The sound of her name made my skin prickle. I did not want to sit with Michael while we both drooled over the same girl. But I couldn't walk away and leave him to fold up on the floor—which was what he looked like he was about to do. "All right," I said.

We took our usual table. Kirby was standing next to Syd's chair at my old table. The girls talked for a few minutes, and then Kirby sat with some kids from my math class.

"Talk to her," Michael said. "About me."

"What?"

"About getting back together."

"I don't think that's such a great idea." Even if I hadn't been lusting after her, there was no way I was getting in the middle of this. "Just tell her yourself."

"She won't listen to me."

"What happened with you two, anyway?"

He stared at her. "I don't know. She said something was missing."

I fought the urge to look in her direction. Michael was gawking enough for both of us. Could she feel his eyes on her?

"She's the only girl I ever loved." He fired the words at me. "And I mean *loved*. I would do anything for her. Climb into a burning building . . . you name the stupid cliché, I would do it."

My stomach stirred. Michael had always been cool and remote with me, but the way he was talking now reminded me of Julia. She got like that sometimes, pulling words from herself as if she were gouging out pieces of her flesh, and flinging them at me. I wanted to stuff my lunch bag in Michael's mouth, tell him I didn't know him well enough for him to say these things. But when I asked myself who did know him well enough, I couldn't come up with anyone.

"You have to talk to her," he said.

"I can't."

"Why not?"

"This is between the two of you."

He finally focused on me. His eyes burned into me, and I remembered how he'd told me he could read faces. I wondered if Kirby's name was written all over mine.

"Sorry," I said.

Michael came up to me after the final bell that afternoon. "Forget what I said at lunch," he said. "Momentary lapse. I'm done with her."

"Okay."

He tapped his fist on the metal of a locker, turned, and walked away.

chapter 16

Nick and Paul came into Barney's on Saturday afternoon while I was working. They sat in my section and made fun of my table-clearing technique for a while. Then Nick said, "Did you hear about Groome?"

"What about him?"

"He tried to chase me and Denise out of Black Mountain Park the other night," Paul said.

"He did that with me and Syd once, too. What's his problem?"

"We thought we'd go by his house tonight."

"And do what?"

Nick shrugged. "Whatever we feel like. You want to come?"

"Maybe." I didn't exactly want to start a war with the Black Mountain kids, but I did hate Groome. And I was so tense over Kirby that I wanted to do *something*. I didn't want to sit home tonight with my little black-and-white TV. So I said, "Yeah, okay."

"Great." He grinned. "Pick you up around eight."

* * *

They picked me up in Nick's car. Nick floored it over to Black Mountain but slowed down on the winding road upward, not wanting the squealing tires to warn everyone we were coming. For a minute I wondered what the hell we were doing. I considered telling them we should turn around. But I kept my mouth shut, and Nick coasted up in front of Groome's house with his headlights off.

You could barely see the house from the road, what with the fifty-mile driveway and all the trees out front. Nick peered out and said, "There's maybe one light on at the house. Might not even be home."

"Let's go see," Paul said, grinning.

Nick turned to me. "You wanna be lookout?"

"All right."

He got out of the car. "Then get up here. Keep the engine running, and if you see anyone turn into the driveway, honk."

I got into the driver's seat while Nick and Paul crept up the driveway. I waited and waited, the Black Mountain night rustling around me. I kept the radio off so I could hear whatever happened, but all I heard was the hum of the engine and the wind in the trees. You couldn't see any other houses from where I was, just the pillars of the driveway entrance across the street. I thought of the Melvilles' driveway, farther up Black Mountain Road, but I let that thought skim off the surface of my mind. I couldn't afford to think about that now.

The Vernons lived even farther up the road. I'd been in their house twice, both times when nobody else was home. The first time, Julia had snuck me in on a freezing January night. ("Thank God everyone's away; we'd turn into Popsicles in that car," she'd said.) She danced around the house—shutting off the alarm system, checking phone messages, and putting her coat away—while I stood in the middle of the living room, staring. Not only was this one room as big as my whole house, but it was spotless. The couch was white and the carpet was this light pink color, and it was clear nobody had ever worn their muddy boots here after walking down by the river, or cleaned a gun on the coffee table, or stuck their feet on the sofa while watching TV. The carpet looked like it had just been installed that morning.

"Hey," Julia said, reappearing in front of me. "Welcome to the Vernon house." She kissed me and slid her hands down my body, but for once I couldn't respond to her. "What's wrong?"

"I don't know. Give me a minute."

"We're not used to having so much room." She laughed. "We can go sit in the car if you'd rather."

"I think we can manage." It wasn't the amount of room that bothered me, but the whole dead chill of the place. The lack of magazines lying around, or cigarette butts in the ashtray, or empty cans on the end tables—the lack of any signs of life.

"Good," she said, pulling her shirt over her head.

"Wait," I said.

"For what?"

The thought of getting naked in that sterile living room, on that stark white couch, was too much. "I want to see your room."

"All right." Smiling, she took my hand and led me down the hall.

I'd hoped this room would have more of Julia in it. And it did: her blue and green bedspread, her clothes flung on one of the chairs, her shelves full of books. But it also had pictures of her with Austin Chadwick all over the dresser.

I guessed she didn't notice the pictures anymore since she saw them every day. She flopped down on her bed. "Come here."

I lay down beside her.

"You know how many times I've wished you were here?"

"How many?" I needed her to flirt with me, to draw me in. I'd started to thaw, with her half-naked body so near, but I still felt numb.

"At least two and a half." She smirked, batting at my arm. "Fishing for compliments."

I rolled on top of her, picking up the cue, my blood flowing again. "So now that I'm here, what are you going to do about it?"

I cut off the memory right there, pulled myself back to the present, to the road outside Groome's driveway. I put my head down on Nick's steering wheel for a minute. I never should have let myself think about that night at Julia's. What the hell good was that going to do?

I sat up again to listen, but heard nothing. I had begun to itch when finally I saw two shapes coming out of Groome's driveway. I shifted the car into drive. Paul slid into the front and Nick into the back, laughing. "Go!" Nick said. "Get us out of here."

We were down on the flats before Nick told me to pull over.

"What'd you do?" I asked as we changed places.

"Slashed his tires. All four of them."

"Didn't his alarm go off?"

"I guess it wasn't on."

Paul laughed. "Why should it be on? Car's just sitting in the driveway, right outside his nice safe castle. What could go wrong?"

"I wish I could see his face tomorrow."

Nick drove us to the Higgins Farm Bridge. There was a car parked there already, right where I used to park with Julia.

"What are we doing here?" I asked.

"Partying!"

We got out, and I recognized the car as Fred's mother's. Fred and Syd came over to us while we unloaded bottles from Nick's trunk.

Nick told us every detail of the tire slashing. He mimicked the way he'd crept around the car in the dark, and even opened his knife to show us. Every time he told the story, his gestures got bigger, his walk stealthier.

"Groome deserves it," Fred said. "You should've keyed the car, too. And sugared the gas tank."

"And smashed the windows," Syd said. I'd never thought of her as the violent type, but now I wondered if Groome's chasing us out of the park had bothered her more than she'd admitted. I tried to catch her eye, but she wouldn't look at me.

I sat on the hood of Nick's car with my bottle while the others stood around in a circle. I was far enough away from them that I didn't have to join the conversation, but close enough to hear everything. I liked it that way sometimes, listening and not having to talk. I hadn't gotten drunk in a long time, and tonight I wanted to. Between our revenge against Groome and the sloshing sound of the river and the comfortable loose feeling I was getting from the bottle, I figured it was a pretty good night.

Syd drifted away from the others and came to me, carrying a plastic cup of wine. She always had wine, since she hated the taste of beer and didn't trust the stronger stuff. "Can I talk to you?" she said.

"Sure."

She looked over her shoulder. Fred was laughing with Nick and Paul. "In here," she said, and opened the back door of Nick's car.

I put my bottle on the ground and slid inside with her. I had the strangest feeling, being at the bridge in the back of a car with a girl. But Nick's car smelled of cigarettes and wet dog. And Syd wasn't Julia.

"I need to talk to someone," she said. "Are we still friends?"

"That's up to you."

She nodded. Then she said, "I screwed up."

"Screwed up how?"

She tilted her head in Fred's direction. "Do you know why I'm with him?"

"Because you like him?"

"Because *he* likes *me*. And I really needed someone to like me, after my dad left and you dumped me."

It took me a minute to absorb that, to feel the sting in it. "Look, Syd, I'm sorry about what happened with us."

"I know you are." She took a swallow of wine. "Just like I'm sorry about what I'm going to do to him. 'Oops, sorry, I don't love you after all.'"

I looked out at Fred again. I was thinking that someone should probably give him a drink. And then I remembered he was driving. Too bad. He was going to wish he had a few drinks in him.

"I've been trying to find a way to do it all night."

Her words rubbed against my nerves. They brought back Julia's words, her constant vows to break up with Austin. I shifted in my seat.

"Sorry for spilling my guts like this," Syd went on.

"No problem." I stuffed thoughts of Julia into a dark closet in the back of my mind.

"I just wanted to talk to you again. I miss you."

"I miss you, too."

She leaned her head against my shoulder. I put an arm around her.

"Fred's going to be okay," she said. "Right?"

"Yeah."

"Did Nick leave his keys in the ignition?" she asked.

"I can't see from here. Why, you planning to steal his car?"

She laughed. "Maybe. I would love to get the hell out of here."

"And go where?"

"Does it matter?"

"Well, that plan's only good if you don't have to come back."

She closed her eyes. "I'm so tired," she said. "I could fall asleep right here."

"Fine with me."

Someone pounded on the roof and windows then, yelling, "OO-HOO!" The car shook. We sat up. Syd's wine splashed onto my knee and the floor. Paul had his face pressed to one window, Nick to the other. Then Nick vanished and Fred was there, yanking open the door on Syd's side.

"What the fuck?" he said.

"They're being idiots," Syd said. "Colt and I were just talking."

"Get out of the car," he said, and ground his teeth so loudly even I could hear it.

"When I'm ready," she said, but she climbed out. Fred leaned in toward me.

"What the fuck, Morrissey?"

"Nothing's going on," I said. I couldn't help thinking of all those times I'd been here with Julia and never been caught, and now here I was caught for something I didn't even do.

"What the *fuck*, Morrissey? You had your chance with her. It's over. You got that? *Over!*"

Paul and Nick hung on to the car, watching and letting out the occasional hoot. I knew they didn't believe for a minute that anything had happened between Syd and me. They obviously thought the whole thing was hilarious, including Fred's raging fit. And Fred wouldn't have believed it either, if half his brain had been working.

"Relax," I said, at the same time Syd told him, "Calm down."

"Don't tell me to relax! Get out here so I can kick your ass."

I got out and stood over him, and he hesitated. He didn't actually step away, but he pulled his head back a couple of inches. I locked on his eyes and said, "Nothing. Happened."

He whirled and stomped off. Syd gave Nick a shove. "What's wrong with you?" she said.

He giggled. "Why, what?"

She rolled her eyes and walked over to Fred.

"Thanks a lot, Nick," I said.

"What, you wanted me to send Fred in there with you? Three-some?"

He was hopelessly drunk. I left him and went to get my own bottle back. Paul sat on the hood of Nick's car. I climbed up next to him.

Nick sat beside us, chuckling. "Things are finally getting interesting." He looked toward the shadows beneath the bridge, where Syd and Fred huddled.

"Nothing happened, and you know it." I shoved him off the car with my foot. He lay in the mud, laughing.

Paul peered over the edge of the hood. "Well, he won't be driving home tonight," he said.

I walked home in the moonlight, stumbling and wandering through the weeds along the riverbank. The river gave off a moldy smell that I happened to like. Even as drunk as I was, I knew my way too well to get lost. I think I was humming. It reminded me of the nights when I used to walk home after meeting Julia at the bridge, only those times I was drunk on her.

The next day I woke up with a headache, my mouth raw and dry. It had been so long since I'd woken up this way that I'd forgotten about this side of partying. I didn't feel like getting out of bed, and when I finally did, I lay around the house until my head stopped pounding. It drove my mother insane. She chased me from room to room, saying, "That's all I need, *two* guys sitting around on their asses," and, "If you're not going to do something with yourself, at least stay the hell out of my way!"

Tom called that afternoon. He told me about his Florida vacation, about the alligators and manatees and herons he'd seen. My brother was probably the only college student in the history of spring break to spend his time at nature preserves instead of the beach. No drunken bikini watching for Tom—or in his case, Speedo watching.

"You want to talk to Mom or Dad?" I asked him before we hung up.

"Oh, Dad, yeah. I'm up for a heart-warming chat."

"What about Mom?"

"Just tell her I said hi. I've got to run."

I went to work as soon as I got off the phone. It was a good thing my job didn't use much of my brain, because Kirby filled my head all night. Either I was going to drive myself crazy or I was going to have to call her. I did call her on my break, but I got her voice mail and didn't feel like leaving a message, so I hung up.

chapter 17

On Monday at school, I looked for Kirby. Whenever I saw her, my blood turned to lava. I had forgotten all those lessons I learned with Julia, about staying detached and burying heat deep underground. But then, it had been months since I'd wanted any girl this much.

At lunch I escaped outside. The yard was finally turning green, and I no longer had it all to myself, but luckily nobody I knew came out today. I didn't want to face Michael or Fred. I would've liked to see Kirby, but I still hadn't decided what to say to her. Or whether to say anything.

Syd came over that afternoon. We sat together on the back-porch steps. It was the first time she'd been at my house since Thanksgiving weekend.

"I guess you heard about me and Fred," she said.

"Nick said you broke up."

She picked up a dried leaf that had fallen onto the porch and twirled the stem between her fingers. "Yeah. I wish it hadn't ended that way, fighting like that. But it had to end somehow. He was suffocating me." She began to split the leaf along the central vein. I watched her peel it apart, then drop the two halves.

"At least you didn't drag it out."

"It's weird, because even though he was getting on my nerves, and it was a mistake for me to go out with him in the first place—I still miss him." She met my eyes, then glanced away. "It's like, once you've gone out with someone, there's a special feeling you have. Even if you never want to go out with them again."

"Yeah," I said. "I know."

She looked around the yard at the weeds, and the gray patches where the rusting wrecks used to lie, and my brother's wooden tower. She sighed and said, "It's good to be back."

"You want to shoot? I could set up the targets."

"Okay."

I was glad to have her talking to me again. After all, we'd been friends since first grade. I liked her back then because she was the only girl who would climb to the top of the monkey bars. We used to sit there with the wind blowing our hair around, thinking we were up so high. To us it was Mount Everest.

On Saturday I went for a walk on the river trail. When I got to the bridge, I crossed under it and kept walking south. Kirby was there, sitting on one of the boulders. I climbed up and sat next to her. The breeze blew her hair into her mouth.

"It's good to see you," she said.

"You, too."

"Where've you been lately? I couldn't find you at lunch."

Did that mean she'd been looking for me? "I've been eating outside."

"Oh."

The sun glare off the river made us squint and look away from it. And whenever we looked away, we glanced at each other, but we didn't let our eyes meet. I stared at a dead snag, the silver skeleton of a tree, on the riverbank. It was a perfect perch for an eagle, though no eagles sat there today. Thinking about eagles kept me from thinking too much of the dream I'd had about Kirby last week. I was glad she couldn't read my mind, but I wondered if she could sense something.

"Want to walk up to the waterfall?" she asked.

"I guess we could."

But we didn't move. The sun heated our faces and the rock we were sitting on. She brushed a strand of hair away from her lips. I kept staring at her mouth and wondering if she noticed. She tilted her face toward the sky and closed her eyes. That made it easier to talk to her. "I called you last weekend," I finally said.

"Really? I didn't get the message."

"I didn't leave one."

She opened her eyes and looked at me. "Why not?"

"I don't know. I guess I wanted to talk to you in person."

"What about?"

"Nothing much. I just wanted to say hi."

"Hi," she said, grinning at me.

I focused on the river until it blinded me, until the sun glare left purple spots in my vision. That was good; I couldn't see her expression when I looked back at her and said, "You're driving me crazy."

She said, "Well, good. Then we're even."

Now I *wanted* to see past the purple spots and couldn't. "What?"

She laughed. "Don't act so surprised, Colt. I thought it was kind of obvious, what was happening between us." She brushed her black hair out of her face. "But I wanted to make sure you were over Julia. I don't want to compete with a dead girl."

"Well, I don't want to compete with Michael."

She waved a hand. "You know that's over. We're friends now." She paused. "One reason we broke up was the way I felt about you. It wasn't fair to Michael, to keep seeing him when I was attracted to somebody else."

"Does he know that?"

"No. There were other reasons, too. I don't mean to blame you." She stared out at the river. "So you still haven't told me you're over Julia."

"I am." I had finished Julia's notebook; I'd read Pam's letter. There was nothing left. "Lately, all I can think about is you."

Kirby smiled and looked back at me. I leaned forward and put my mouth on hers. Kissing her was like diving into black water.

For a week after that, I was so wrapped up in Kirby that I hardly noticed anything else. We ate lunch together at school. We talked on the phone every night when I got off work.

I did wonder how Michael was going to take it, seeing Kirby with me, but he didn't have much of a reaction. He just nodded, as if he'd seen us together thousands of times before. As if he'd never mentioned running into a burning building for her, or asked me to help him get her back. I hoped he'd meant it when he'd called that a momentary lapse, when he'd told me he was done with her.

Syd was the other person I worried about, even though she'd told me when she broke up with Fred that things were okay between us now. The first time she saw me with Kirby, her face went blank for a few seconds, and I couldn't tell what she was thinking, but then she relaxed. She talked to both Kirby and me without any edge in her voice.

Kirby came over on Friday night. To get ready for her, I threw my dirty clothes into the basement and kicked some empty cans and old homework papers into the closet. I put fresh sheets on the bed. Then I lay on the mattress, smelling the clean sheets and imagining Kirby's skin against their cool whiteness. Not that I was sure I'd get to see that, but it was nice to think about.

I looked at the water stain that had crept across my ceiling and tried to count the months since I'd last had a girl in my room. There was Syd, but we'd been friends for so long, and she'd seen my room so many times, that I'd never made any special preparations for her. And Julia had never been here at all.

After I'd been to Julia's house, she'd hinted about coming to mine. I didn't see how we could manage it because Tom was too unpredictable, often changing his mind at the last minute about whether he was going out or staying home. I couldn't imagine Julia in my room anyway.

Sometimes she had driven me home from the bridge. One spring night she pulled up in front of my house and teased, "Should I come in?"

"Thanks for the ride," I said, opening my door. But she put her hand on my arm.

"I'm just kidding. You don't have to get so nervous. What, are you running an illegal casino in there or something?"

"Yeah. Don't tell anyone or we'll have to kill you." I gave her a quick kiss, but before I could climb out of the car, she spoke again.

"I don't expect you to have marble floors and chandeliers in every room. I'm not stupid, you know."

I got out and came around to her side. She rolled down the window, and I said, "Yeah, that's why I don't want you in my house. Because we only have chandeliers in half the rooms."

She opened her mouth to respond, then shook her head. "See you next Friday."

I reached in the window and grabbed her wrist. "Come in then."

She kept her hands on the steering wheel. "No, forget it."

"You wanted to, so come on in." I wasn't sure who was calling whose bluff at this point, but I could tell from the way her hands clamped on the wheel that she was not getting out of that car.

"I don't have time tonight."

I released her, and she drove away. She never did come inside. After that night, she never even brought it up again.

My mother was at work and my father was slumped in front of the TV when Kirby arrived. I don't know if Dad even realized Kirby was in the house, although she said hello when she passed him. I took her right into my room.

"So this is Colt Headquarters," she said. "This is where it all happens."

"Yeah, if by 'it all' you mean sleep and homework."

She stopped in front of my TV. "Wow, this looks like the one my grandparents have in their basement. How old is it?"

"Don't ask."

She wandered through the room, reading the titles of the books on my shelves, running her fingers along the edge of my desk. I sat on my bed and watched her, feeling a little like she'd peeled back my skin to touch the bones and muscles inside.

"What's this?" She held up a seashell.

"A shell."

She made a face that said, *Give me some credit.* "I mean, why is this shell, out of all the shells in the world, in your room?"

I leaned back and kicked off my shoes. "My grandparents once took Tom and me to the beach for a week. I was about—nine, I think. It was the only time I ever saw the ocean." As I talked, I could hear the roar of waves against the shore, and taste the salt. I saw the immense stretch of water, more water than I'd ever imagined in my life, water that gave me my first idea of how big the world was. "Tommy piled up a whole bunch of shells. He wanted to bring them home and make things out of them. But Grandma said we should leave them, because animals needed to live in them, and other people would like to see them, too. Tom got so upset that she said we could each take one shell home."

"That's nice," Kirby said, turning the shell over in her fingers. Then she set it back on the shelf.

She asked me about a trophy I had (junior high, relay race). She pulled out a few books. "Oh, I loved this!" (*The Catcher in the Rye.*) "I never got through this." (*Catch-22.*) "Did you like this?" (*Into the Wild.*)

I took a deep breath.

"What?" she said. "It wasn't any good?"

"No, it was good."

"It must be sad." She watched my face, obviously trying to figure out what was bothering me.

"Yeah . . ." I decided to just tell her. After all, I didn't want to make a bigger deal over it than it was. "Julia gave me that."

"Oh." She put it back on the shelf.

"You can borrow it if you want."

"Maybe." She touched the spines of several other books, but didn't ask me about them.

I watched her fingers, touching all these things that were mine, stroking the wood of my shelves and desk, tracing invisible patterns on the furniture. I got up and stood behind her. She went very still, and I put my arms around her. I wanted to kiss her neck, to move my hands up over her chest, but it seemed too soon. I just held her. She settled back into me.

"Where do you want to look next?" I whispered in her ear.

"Hmm . . . there's the closet," she murmured. "I haven't seen that yet."

"Nothing in there. Just some clothes. And some junk I cleared off the floor and crammed in there when I knew you were coming over."

She laughed. "You cleaned up for me."

"Yeah. I even vacuumed."

"Wow, I feel like a queen."

Now I did kiss her neck. She turned around and kissed me. All week, we'd been stealing kisses at school between classes, and in the few minutes between school ending and me leaving for my shift at Barney's. This was the first time we'd been alone together without a clock ticking over our heads.

She broke away for a second to say, "I know where I want to go next."

"I hope it's the same place I want to go."

She led me to the bed.

"Yep," I said, "same place."

We lay down together.

I didn't know how far she'd want to go, where she would draw the lines. I didn't want to draw any lines myself. I tried to focus on what we were doing at the moment and not worry about what was going to happen next.

After we'd made out for a while, long enough for me to lose the sense of where my mouth ended and hers began, she took off her shirt and bra. I got up to lock my door and take off my shirt. When I came back to bed, as soon as I touched her, she shivered.

"You cold?"

"No." All the time shuddering, as I ran my hand down her bare arm.

"Do you—want to stop?"

"No."

We never did stop.

Everything I'd felt for her the day of the snowstorm, the day I showed her the waterfall, the day I first kissed her on the rocks by the river, boiled up and boiled over. Afterward, as we lay there catching our breath, still wrapped around each other, I said, "I love you." I hadn't planned to say it. I just opened my mouth and it came out.

"Um, you don't have to say that now," she joked. "I've already slept with you."

"I mean it."

She rolled on top of me then, her long black hair sweeping over my face and neck, and she put her mouth next to my ear, and she said it. It went right into my head, her breath and the words, filling my ear and filling me up.

chapter 18

I was scheduled to work on Sunday morning. When I came out of the house, I found my mother's tires gashed open.

I walked all the way around the car and then stood in the driveway for a minute, staring at the damage. Somehow I'd expected this. I'd always known somebody would pay for that night at Groome's. Groome was not the type to just swallow and take it.

I went back to the house and called Nick, waking him up.

"What the hell?" he yawned.

"Hey, Nick, how are your tires?"

"My what?"

"Your *tires.* On your car."

"Why?"

"I'd check them if I were you."

"Hold on." After a couple of minutes, he was back. "Shit!"

"All four?"

"Hell, yeah. You, too?"

"Yep. You better call Paul. I have to find another way to work."

"Shit. Groome is going to pay for this."

"I guess he considered it payback," I said.

"How did he know it was us?"

"We didn't exactly keep it a secret." I checked the clock. "I've got to go, Nick. I'll talk to you later."

I called Sunil, who was on the same shift as me, and he agreed to give me a ride. I left a note for my mother about the car. I was glad I wouldn't be there when she read it.

Mom still hadn't calmed down by the time I got home. "This is one hell of a kick in the ass!" She stalked around the kitchen in her bathrobe, emptying the dishwasher. She threw things into drawers, jabbing at me occasionally with a spoon or a spatula. "You know our insurance doesn't cover this."

The rock in my stomach got heavier. "It doesn't?"

"Hell, no. That car's such a piece of junk anyway, it wasn't worth it to get full coverage." She pointed a fork at me. "You're paying for two of those tires. You wanted the responsibility of driving, this is part of it."

"I know." Really I should be paying for all four, but how could I tell her that without telling her about Groome's tires? She'd kill me. "I have the money."

"Do you know what new tires *cost*?" She slammed a drawer shut. "Idiot kids, probably. Think it's funny to slash tires. I'd like to wring their stupid necks."

"Mom, I—"

"Do they know how long I've got to stand on my feet to earn those tires? Christ. As if I didn't have better things to spend the money on. Like food."

"Mom—"

"Oh, go study or something. You're in my way."

I got to my room as the phone rang. I picked up my extension and heard Nick's voice.

"This is war," he said.

Paul's tires hadn't been touched, but Fred's had. This told us that Groome had less than perfect information. He didn't know that Paul was involved, he didn't know that Fred wasn't, and he couldn't have been completely sure about Nick and me. Not that that stopped him from taking his revenge.

"I've had it with Black Mountain," Nick told me on the phone. "Adam Hancock taking my parking space because he thinks Black Mountain guys own that end of the lot. Austin Chadwick looking at me like I'm some piece of shit he stepped in. Groome's just the worst one. This Friday night, we're going up there to the park, and take over."

I thought Nick had been watching too many movies. "The four of us are going to take over a mountain? With what?"

"What do you mean, four? I'm talking about *all* the kids from the flats. We're sick of this shit." He raved on, describing in detail what he wanted to do to Groome's car, face, and internal organs.

"Wait," I interrupted. "How many people are in this with you?"

"Everybody. You, me, Paul, Fred . . . and Ryan Coates, and Jimmy Reilly, and Mike Dunn . . . and each one of them is telling ten more people. We'll have every kid in the flats up there."

More people must've been hassled by Groome and Chadwick than I'd thought. Either that, or these guys didn't fully understand what Nick had in mind. "You sure they don't all think this is just a big party?"

"It'll be a party, all right. Friday night," Nick said. "You can ride with me."

"I want to go with you," Kirby said.

We were at the river, sitting on our boulder, the spot where I'd first kissed her. It was Wednesday, one of the few afternoons that I didn't have to work. "Kirby, I'm not even sure I'm going." I hadn't made up my mind about Friday night on Black Mountain. After all, Nick's last bright idea had gotten me four slashed tires.

"You're going. I know you. And I want to be there."

"Why? It's not your fight."

"What's that supposed to mean?"

"You don't live on the flats."

"Well, I sure don't live on the mountain," she said.

"It could get ugly."

"It's already gotten ugly."

I sighed. She had an answer for everything.

"Don't give me any crap about how I'm a helpless girl who needs to be protected," she said.

"I wasn't going to. But I don't want you to get hurt."

"I won't." She tossed a strand of hair out of her face. "I'm not asking your permission, anyway. If Nick won't let me come in his car, I'll take my mother's. Or walk."

"What are you going to tell your Black Mountain friends if you show up in Nick's car with us?"

"What do you mean?"

I rubbed my hand on the rough stone beneath us. "Going out with me is bad enough. You come to the park with us Friday night, and I don't think they'll be taking you to the country club anymore."

She snorted. "You think they *ever* invite me to the country club? Or to their parties, now that Pam's gone?"

"I've seen you eat lunch at Austin's table."

"Yeah, and Julia used to act like I was this huge annoyance whenever I'd dare to sit there. Even when I was going out with Michael, they still treated me like an outsider. And now you tell me I don't belong with you guys, either, because I don't live on the flats." She stared out at the river. "Nick always looks at me funny, like I'm a spy from Black Mountain. Nobody trusts me, not you and not them."

"I trust you."

"Good, then you'll let me come with you."

"I don't know, Kirby."

"Well, I'm going up there, Colt, with or without you." She stood. "Come on, let's go walk someplace. I'm sick of sitting around."

chapter 19

Nick picked me up on Friday night. Paul was already in the car. We stopped on the way to get Kirby.

Cars streamed up the mountain, lights flashing, horns honking. Paul rolled down the window and stuck his head out. Nick laughed at nothing. Kirby shivered. Something sizzled and sparked in the air; we all felt it.

"Where's Fred?" I asked.

"He's going in Ryan's car."

"Is Syd coming?"

"No."

I was glad to hear that. If the Black Mountain kids decided to fight with us, she wouldn't want to be there. Nick had spread the word that anyone from Black Mountain should stay away from the park tonight, so of course we expected some of them to show up.

I wondered what Julia would've thought of all this. Kirby had told me that Michael thought it was completely moronic, that this whole thing was driven by Nick and Groome showing off. Julia would have thought so, too. "The only time Austin ever looks for a fight is when he listens to Keith Groome's bullshit," she'd written in her notebook. But at the same time, she loved excitement. She probably would've come, if only to see what happened.

The park had a long, narrow parking lot. Usually people pulled into the spaces headfirst, facing the view off the mountain. Tonight we backed in, thinking we could pull out fast in case of trouble. We got one of the last places in the lot, but cars kept coming after us. They parked in the grass; they stopped in the roadway. They piled in, honking, until we couldn't have pulled out if we'd wanted to.

"What do we do now?" Paul asked.

"Wait," Nick said, grinning.

So far everyone just seemed to be sitting in their cars, radios cranked up, engines racing. It took me a few minutes to realize the cars didn't all belong to kids from the flats. I saw Austin's car, and Groome's, and Adam Hancock's, and Tristan Allen's. I'd expected to see more of the Black Mountain guys, and I wondered if the others had stayed away because they were scared or because they thought the whole thing was stupid. After all, the park would always belong to them, no matter what happened tonight.

Chadwick and Groome and those guys were parked on the grass near the entrance, next to a sign that told people to clean up after their dogs. The closest flats cars faced them, separated by a space of grass. That space of grass was the DMZ, I told myself. No-man's land.

We'd been sitting there about twenty minutes when Austin got out of his car. He walked across the DMZ, heading toward the nearest flats car, but Brad Letts climbed out of it and met him on the grass. When they got close enough to each other, their mouths opened wide. They must've been yelling, but we couldn't hear over all the engines and radios. They shoved each other. Then they backed off, yelling and flailing their arms. Letts beckoned Austin with a "come over here" hand wave.

Groome got out of his car. At the sight of him, about five kids from the flats jumped out and went after him. Paul ran to join in. Adam Hancock and Tristan Allen had enough sense, or fear, to stay inside their cars.

"God," Kirby said, "six against one? That's too much."

"Yeah," Nick said, "but are you going to stop them?"

We couldn't even see Groome anymore, just a knot of people pushing and punching and kicking, and what they were punching and kicking seemed to be down on the ground now. Kids from the flats were out of their cars by this time, standing on hoods and roofs. Someone jumped up on Hancock's gleaming silver car and began to bounce on it. More kids jumped onto Groome's car, and Ryan Coates bashed Groome's windshield with a rock.

Austin turned to look, and all of a sudden he must've realized what the odds were, because he yelled one last thing at Letts and ran back to his car. He reached into it, got something, and held it up. He stood there holding his arm up like the Statue of Liberty, screaming at the guys attacking Groome.

"What's he saying?" Nick asked.

"He's threatening to call the police," Kirby said. "That's his cell phone."

Paul ran up, ripped the phone out of Austin's hand, and threw it away. They exchanged punches—Paul's missed—and then Austin scrambled into his car. Paul returned to the knot around Groome, but the guys were already backing off, leaving Groome crawling on the ground.

"This is awful," Kirby said. She got out, went over to Groome, and knelt beside him. The air was full of honking and hooting and cheering. Maybe Austin hadn't been able to call the cops, but I figured they'd be here soon anyway. I doubted that the rich people who lived around here would put up with this noise much longer.

I opened my door. I didn't want Kirby to be alone out there. Nick said, "Colt, are you crazy?"

"This is what you wanted, isn't it? Why the hell don't you come out, too?"

He stayed behind the wheel. I almost said something about him starting this whole thing, only to hide when the blood started flowing. But I didn't want to get into it with Nick now.

I went over to Kirby. Paul and those guys were telling her to leave Groome alone, but she ignored them. Groome groaned, and the way he moved reminded me of the way a bug moves when you've crushed it but not quite killed it. There was so much blood I could smell it, a smell like hot metal. Most of it poured from his nose.

"God, Colt," Kirby said, "is there a towel or something in Nick's car?"

I walked back to Nick. He usually had a beach towel or a blanket in his trunk. "As far as I'm concerned, the guy can bleed to death," he said.

"Look, Nick, he's pretty banged up."

"That's too damn bad. He should've thought of that before he slashed my tires." Nick craned his neck to look past me. "Ahh, he'll be okay. Kirby's overreacting. I knew we shouldn't have brought her."

I went back to Kirby. Paul bent down to get a closer look at Groome. "Whoa," he said. Kirby and I used my jacket to stop the blood, though I gritted my teeth when I handed it over. I noticed that Groome had wet his pants, a dark stain spreading over his crotch and down his legs.

Austin stood over us, shouting at the guys who'd attacked Groome, until Kirby yelled, "Shut up! You're not helping." Then she said to Paul, "Can you calm those guys down?"

The rest of the guys who'd beaten up Groome were still milling around, rubbing their knuckles, itching to take on Austin and anyone else who might dare to step out of their cars. Paul got them to back off a little. Most of the other kids in the park were standing on their cars, watching, quieter now. Groome's blood seemed to have satisfied some appetite.

"Maybe you should go to the emergency room," Kirby told Groome. "Your nose might be broken."

"Fuck that," he said, although through his mashed nose and the cloth of my jacket it sounded more like "Huck dat."

"He'll be okay." Austin leaned over and slapped Groome's shoulder. "Right, buddy?"

Cars were leaving, as if there was nothing more to stay for, now that the violence was over. Tristan Allen and Adam Hancock came up and helped Groome into the backseat of Austin's car. Austin shut the car door and turned to us.

"You guys have gone too fucking far," he said. "Tell all your friends, you guys are going to be paying for Groome's car until you get so old your fucking dicks fall off." He pointed at me. "You got that, Colt Fucking Morrissey?"

I hadn't thought he even knew my name. I knew plenty about him, but I'd always believed that was a one-way street. To him, I was just a guy from the flats. A nobody. It would make sense that he'd hate me if he'd known about Julia, but he couldn't have known. Could he?

"You're welcome, Austin," Kirby said, her voice full of venom.

"Hey, Kirby, don't take it the wrong way. You've always been okay with me, and what you did tonight shows it. I just don't know why you want to hang out with this loser."

"Oh, go to hell," Kirby said. She turned away from him, and Austin looked at me again.

"What were you trying to prove, coming up here?" he said.

I didn't answer. I followed Kirby.

By this time, there were hardly any cars left. As we crossed the empty lot back to Nick's car, we both started to shiver. I put my arm around her and she said, "I'm glad you helped with Keith. I'll say thank you even if they won't."

I did it for you, not them, I thought. But I didn't say it out loud.

Nick rolled down the window and said, "I'm not so sure I want her in this car."

Kirby glared at him. "Why not?"

"I don't know why you had to run over and help that asshole and ruin everything."

"They could've killed him, Nick! It's not like on TV, where a guy can take fifty punches and walk away. This is serious."

"Colt, you getting in?"

"Not unless you let Kirby in, too."

"Fine. You can both walk." He started the engine and yelled, "See ya!"

Nick tore out of there, and Kirby and I sat on the grass. The cold dew soaked into my jeans. Kirby sniffed and ran the heel of one hand beneath her eyes. Her hand was splotched with Groome's blood. "I never cry," she said sharply.

"We'll be okay," I said. "We can walk home." I picked up her hands; they felt cold and dead. I rubbed them to get her blood flowing again. "Hey, if the police come roaring up here now, at least we'll have a ride home."

My lame attempt at humor did nothing to cheer her up. "Do you think like Nick?" she asked. "Do you think I should've stayed out of it?"

"No."

"You know this is serious, right? Keith could get people arrested if he wanted."

"Yes."

"Talk to me, Colt. I can't stand these one-word answers."

I squeezed her cold fingers. "I think we'd better start walking so you can warm up. It's a long way." If I had been alone in the backseat of Nick's car tonight, I never would've gone to help Groome. I would've sat back and watched him get killed. "I think you did the right thing. I think you're a better person than I am."

I wanted to tell her I loved her, too, but somehow I couldn't. The words rose up to the back of my tongue and stuck there. Ever since I'd said them that night in my room, I hadn't been able to get them out of my mouth again. I didn't know why.

■ *chapter 20* ■

We walked down to Kirby's, and she drove me from there. I got home around one in the morning. My father's snoring filled the house. I took a shower to get the blood and dirt off me, and then I crept into my room.

I couldn't sleep. My mind was a jumble of smashed glass, and howls, and Groome's blood. Over and over, I heard Austin saying, "What were you trying to prove?"

I rolled around in bed for a while, but I kept itching, or getting an ache in my arm, or tangling the sheets. I turned the light back on and dug Julia's notebook out of my desk drawer.

I hadn't read it since I'd first started thinking about Kirby. After all, I had finished it. I'd moved on, left Julia behind.

I told myself all this, and then I paged through the book, looking for an entry I remembered, one that Julia had written in the middle of an April night.

Dear C.M.,

I couldn't sleep, so I decided to get up and write. I wrote a poem, but I'm not tired yet.

I was thinking about college. It's hard to believe I only have one more year at home. After that I'll be at Harvard (I hope!), and at some point, I definitely want to do a year in Europe. France, I think.

It doesn't seem real. My plans sound big, but how do I know I can live up to them? My life has always been Black Mountain and the Willis River and this stupid little town. My stepfather works in the city, and so does Austin's dad. They think of this town as a quiet place to come home to after they've spent all day in the "real world." I'll bet nobody outside this county has even heard of Black Mountain.

Maybe a school like Harvard would eat me alive. Maybe I won't get in. Reality is going to smack a lot of Black Mountain kids in the face when they graduate. Keith Groome thinks he's going to Princeton, but with the grades he's got I don't think Princeton would let him mow their lawns.

I wish I could talk to you right now.

I might even try to call, if it weren't two thirty in the morning.

What do you think about when you can't sleep? Sometimes I think about the ocean. I can see it lapping on the shore, waves rolling in one after the other, washing over the sand, never stopping. That's what usually puts me to sleep.

I decided it couldn't hurt to try. I called up the rhythm of the waves from that one time I'd seen the ocean. That got me calmer, even sleepy, but it didn't take enough of the edge off. I knew a way I could definitely fall asleep, and I tried to think about Kirby, but it didn't help.

What worked, finally, was thinking about Julia. I told myself it wasn't really like cheating on Kirby. I tried like hell to think about Kirby instead. But for some reason, tonight it was Julia.

On Saturday I took one of Tom's old jackets out of his bedroom closet and hoped Mom wouldn't ask what had happened to mine. Wearing his jacket reminded me that I hadn't talked to him in a while, and I called him at school.

"Colt! You're actually calling me? What, did the house burn down or something?"

"Very funny. No, I thought you'd want to hear about last night."

"What about it?"

I told him what had happened. "So, what do you think?"

He paused. "I forgot about all that Black Mountain bullshit. You don't let it get to you, do you?"

"No."

"I remember people saying the word 'flats' like it was a synonym for 'toxic waste dump.' Just wait till you leave that town and see how small Black Mountain really is."

Julia's letter last night had said the same thing. "I know."

"Once you're out here in the world, nobody cares where you used to live. Who you are, that's what counts."

"Uh-huh. Should I be humming inspiring background music while you're giving this speech?"

He laughed. "Okay, I know my cue to shut up."

"Then I guess there's a first time for everything."

"Ooh, little brother's getting a bit too full of himself! Sounds like someone needs to come back and put him in his place."

"When are you coming home, anyway?"

"Not until after finals." He took the phone away and said to someone else, "Hey, have a seat."

"Who's there?" I asked.

"Uh—Derek just walked in."

Something in the way he said that name told me what was coming. "Derek?"

"Yeah, this guy I've been seeing."

It's one thing to know your brother is gay in the abstract, but to think of him with a real live boyfriend is—strange, kind of. I mean, it takes getting used to. "You sure you wouldn't rather just screw around?"

He laughed. "Yeah, that's tempting, but I think I want to be with Derek for a while."

Someone in the background—Derek, I guessed—yelled, "'For a while!' Great! It's almost like a commitment!"

"I should let you go," I said.

"Talk to you later."

After I hung up, I thought of what he'd said about Black Mountain. It was true in a way. I knew it was small compared to the rest of the world. But I figured there were more Black Mountains beyond the one in our town. Bigger ones, too.

Kirby might have thought she was caught in the middle before, but that was nothing compared to the week after the fight at Black Mountain Park. Everyone hated her. The Black Mountain kids wouldn't talk to her because she'd been with us that night. The kids from the flats wouldn't talk to her because she'd helped Groome. Her locker became a dumping ground, with people sticking things through the vents. (Some of it we couldn't identify—just like busing tables at Barney's.) She moved her books and coat into my locker.

She would've gotten even worse treatment if she had been completely isolated. But three people stuck by her: Syd, Michael, and me.

The four of us ate lunch together that week, forming a little island that nobody else would come near. Syd pretended she didn't care. Michael didn't have to pretend; he obviously didn't care what anyone else thought of him. I didn't like Michael spending so much time with Kirby, but I thought it was important that somebody from Black Mountain was sticking up for her.

"Adam and some other guys drive by my house every night, honking," Kirby said while we ate our sandwiches. "We've had so many hang-up calls, we've taken the phone off the hook."

"Ignore them," Syd said.

"They'll get sick of it," Michael said. "This weekend there's another country-club party. That'll take their minds off you."

"Great," Kirby said. "Then I just have to worry about the guys from the flats."

"I've been talking to Nick," Syd told her. "I finally convinced him enough is enough. The only one who still doesn't want to let things drop is Ryan Coates." Groome hadn't called the police on anybody, but he was making noises about getting Ryan back for the smashed windshield. I think he cared more about the car than he did about his face.

"How did Groome keep the cops out of this, anyway?" I said. Even my parents would've insisted on an explanation if I'd come home looking like he did that night.

"He told his father that it was a fight, and the other guy got the worst of it," Michael said. "He didn't have to tell his mother anything. She's in France with her latest boy toy."

"His father believed that story?"

"Brains don't exactly run in the family. Testosterone, on the other hand—"

"What about the car?"

"It's at the garage," Syd said. "Apparently Keith told his father something about hitting a post."

"Hitting a post," I repeated, and scratched the back of my neck.

She laughed. "Yeah, I know. Like Michael said, the Groomes aren't known for their brains. And since Keith's father never actually saw the car, I guess he didn't question it. Anyway, Keith is trying to get the money out of Ryan Coates."

"Why doesn't he just smash Coates's windshield and get it over with?" I said.

"Like he slashed your tires?" Michael said, with a superior smile. "A tire for a tire, a windshield for a windshield?"

"God, let's talk about something else," Kirby said.

Groome walked past my table in study hall. The second I glanced up, he shot out, "What are you looking at?"

The beating he'd taken hadn't changed his attitude. The fact that I'd used my own jacket to soak up his blood didn't seem to matter to him either. I was beginning to think Kirby and I should've let him bleed to death. I looked at the bruises on his face—red and purple, black and yellow—and smiled. "I like what you've done with your face, Groome."

"You better watch yourself, Morrissey."

"You threatening me? Maybe next time it won't be just your tires that get cut up."

"Watch yourself," he repeated, and stomped away.

On Saturday night, I worked at Barney's. It was the first warm night we'd had this spring, and I kept drifting near the door to try to catch the breeze from outside. "Colten! Get back to your station! And smile!" Al told me.

Around eleven, during the pie-and-coffee hours, a whole crowd of Black Mountain kids came in. They were dressed up, the way Julia had been that first night, and half-drunk and noisy. I remembered Michael talking about a country-club party tonight. They must've come from there.

They sat in my section. Austin stood in the aisle, face pink and eyes glazed, his chest out. When I tried to get around him, he said, "You want to take over our spots, we're going to take over yours." It took me a minute to realize what he meant: They were coming to Barney's because we'd gone to Black Mountain Park.

Well, that was a fair exchange, I thought, since the park was a hell of a lot nicer than Barney's Steakhouse. In fact, if Austin would say the word, I'd be happy to move into his mansion and drive his car.

I set their tables for them. That was humiliating enough, until they started saying things like, "Oh, my napkin's a little crooked. Could you straighten it for me?" Or they'd throw their silverware on the floor and say, "Oops. Dropped my fork. Could you get me another one?"

After I'd brought them about three times more silverware than they ever should've needed, I sent Sunil over to them. He kept his perpetual smile, no matter how many times they changed their orders or asked stupid questions like, "The blueberry pie, what kind of berries does it have?"

They lit cigarettes. "Excuse me, no smoking please, thank you," Sunil said. One person would put out a cigarette, and then another would light up, and they'd go through the whole routine again. Then they started pretending they couldn't understand Sunil's English.

"Excuse me? What's that you said?" Big cloud of smoke in Sunil's face. "Where you from, anyway?"

Sunil's face began to gleam with sweat, but he never stopped smiling. Al would've wet his pants with proud joy over that invincible "friendly, welcoming" smile.

When the orders were ready, Sunil beckoned me into the kitchen. "You know these people?"

"They're Black Mountain shit. Why don't you accidentally spill a pot of coffee in someone's lap?"

He clicked his tongue against the roof of his mouth. "No need for that." He peeled back the top crust of one of the pie slices. "But you can spit in their pie."

"What?" For a second, I wasn't sure I'd heard him right. Sunil had never, ever been nasty to a customer, no matter how badly the customer treated him. But he held the pie open for me, and I spat.

"Very good," he said, and patted the crust back into place. I hoped it was Austin's slice. I laughed as Sunil carried it into the dining room. I didn't come out until I could keep a straight face.

I decided I wouldn't clear their table until after they'd left, but there was a table near theirs I had to clean off. While I was doing it, one of the guys lobbed a lump of pie crust at me. It hit me in the shoulder. A couple of the other kids laughed, and then a strawberry, coated with gooey pie filling, flew my way. That one splatted on the floor, but another one hit my arm.

We had deep plastic pans to scrape the food waste into, and when I saw more food flying at me, I picked up the pan and caught the scraps. I didn't think about it; it was kind of a reflex. After all, I didn't want the food to land on me, and I didn't want it to land on the floor, because I was the one who'd have to clean it up.

A couple of them laughed in surprise when I caught the food. One of the girls threw a piece of doughnut, only this time she was aiming for the pan. I moved the pan enough to catch it. And then they were all doing it. It had become a game, with them laughing and pitching food and me catching it. (Well, most of it, anyway.) I didn't know why this had turned from an ugly scene into comedy, but it was all right with me. They were laughing as they picked up their checks—all but Austin. He still scowled at me.

One thing about those rich kids: they tipped big. When Sunil counted up the total, he said, "I'm almost sorry I let you spit in their pie."

chapter 21

On Sunday night, Kirby and I were in my bedroom.
I lay on the bed, more asleep than awake, while she paced the room, naked. "Wake up, Colt," she teased. Sex always relaxed me, but for some reason it made her restless.

She stopped in front of my desk and flipped open the purple notebook, which I'd forgotten to put away after that night on Black Mountain. "What's this?"

Well, *that* made me sit up. "It's Julia's."

She stared down at the page for another minute, then turned back to me. "Julia's?"

"Yeah. Didn't Michael tell you? That's how he found out about me and her in the first place."

"Right," she said. "He did tell me." She read a page. I wanted to tell her to stop. I wanted to slam the book closed, but I was afraid of where that would take us.

"So why do you still have it?" she asked.

"What do you mean?"

"It's her diary, right? Don't you think her family wants it back?"

I'd never thought of that. The letters were written to me, and they weren't the kind of things most parents would want to read about their own kid. Julia wrote about having sex with me and getting drunk with her friends. She wrote about cheating on Austin—the guy her family loved. Why would they want to see any of that? "No," I said. "Michael's never asked for it back. He didn't even want to read it."

"He told me he showed it to you because Julia would've wanted that. I'm sure he didn't mean for you to keep it."

"You don't care about the Vernons having it," I said. "You just don't want me to have it."

Her mouth twitched. "Even if that's true," she said, "can you blame me?"

I wished she would sit down. Instead she stood there naked, next to my desk. I looked away from her. My underwear lay on the floor. I picked it up and put it on. Kirby just stood there, watching me. I found my jeans and put them on, too.

"Why don't you at least ask Michael if he wants it back?"

"He won't want it," I said. "She wrote it to me."

"You mean the whole thing's like this? 'Dear C.M.,' it's all about you and her?"

I didn't answer.

"God, Colt! Why are you hanging on to it? Even if the Vernons don't want it—get rid of it!"

I didn't want to throw it away or give it back. It surprised me to realize that, because in the two months since I'd finished it, I'd had it sitting in a drawer. I hadn't looked at it again until the other night when I couldn't sleep. "Not now," I said.

"Not *now*? What the hell does that mean?" She slammed the notebook closed. "I told you when we started going out that I wasn't going to compete with a dead girl."

"It's not like that." I walked the floor, kicking at our clothes and shoes and the empty condom wrapper.

"Then what is it like, Colt? Do you love me or not?"

"Yes. You know that."

"How do I know that? Because you said it once in the middle of sex? You'd say anything then."

"It wasn't in the middle," I said, but her face told me that wasn't the point. "Kirby, don't do this."

"Don't do what? I'm supposed to believe you love me when you're clinging to your ex-girlfriend's diary? It's sitting right here on your desk while I'm in bed with you! You know how that makes me feel?" She stormed over to her clothes and started picking them up off the floor. "What is so damn special about Julia anyway? Will you tell me that?"

I knew I could stop this anytime by promising to get rid of the notebook. I kept telling myself to promise that, but the words snagged in my throat. "Kirby, this is crazy. You're the one I want."

"You have a strange way of showing it." She pulled her shirt over her head. "Call me when you get over Julia."

Everyone gradually forgot they were mad at Kirby about the fight at Black Mountain. Groome beat up Ryan Coates because of the windshield, and things went back to normal. Only, between Kirby and me, things weren't normal.

I missed her. I'd wrapped her into my life more than I had any other girl before. Julia might have lived in my head while I was seeing her, but Kirby was in my real life, full-time. We'd only been together a few weeks, but we'd seen each other every day at lunch. And whenever I didn't have to work we walked along the river or hung out in my room or went to the movies. This week, when she wasn't talking to me, I felt like I was walking around with an invisible Kirby next to me. A cold, silent Kirby.

After three days of her avoiding me, I opened the notebook one last time. I read an entry at random, an entry from last July.

> Dear C.M.,
>
> Just lying here listening to music. Pam and I were up at Blueberry Lake all day, and I think I got sunburned. My face has that tight feeling. Everyone was there, Austin and Keith and Tristan and Adam, but I managed to get away for a few minutes and sit under some pines by myself. I love the way pines filter sunlight. I rolled in the needles because they smelled so good. I would've liked to stay under there for hours.
>
> But everybody was waiting for me, looking, calling, and I had to go back to them.

I brought the notebook to school. I handed it to Michael at his locker, between classes.

"What?" he said. "What are you doing?"

"Julia's notebook. Thanks for showing it to me."

"Why are you giving it to me?"

"Well, it's your family's now. I thought you might want it back."

He stared at the book, as if I were trying to hand him a spitting cobra. "All that slop she wrote about you? No thanks."

"Your parents?"

"Are you out of your mind? They love Austin. They wouldn't even want to know you exist."

I slid it back into my stack of books, relieved. He studied my face.

"You know, Morrissey," he said, "Kirby's better than you deserve. Why don't you concentrate on her?"

"I am. Why do you think I'm trying to give back the notebook?"

"I assume it's because it bothers Kirby. She hasn't spoken to you all week."

He was the last person I wanted to talk about Kirby with. "That's none of your business."

"You're a great one, aren't you? Leading her on while you read my sister's notebook. What do you do with it anyway, sleep with it between your legs?" He took a book out of his locker and slammed the door. "Hell, just throw it away." He smiled then, a cold smile, and said, "If you can."

At lunch I told Kirby how I'd tried to give the notebook back, how Michael wouldn't take it. "So what are you going to do with it?" she asked.

"Pack it away somewhere." I didn't want to throw it out. I couldn't just stick it in the trash. I hoped my answer was good enough for Kirby.

She nodded. "Okay."

Syd and Nick came up to our table then. "I can't believe you're actually sitting with me, Nick," Kirby said. "After all, you couldn't even stand to have me in your car."

"Hey, I'll forget about that night if you will."

"Why should I forget it? I didn't do anything wrong."

Syd put her hand on the table between them. "Shut up, both of you."

Kirby gave Nick a dark look—I knew she still thought he should apologize—but she didn't push it.

"Let's go outside," Syd said. "It's beautiful."

Michael joined us as we got up from the table. Everyone went into the hall and headed for the doors at the back of the building. But Kirby took my hand, held me back. Michael looked over his shoulder at us. He didn't say anything, or even blink, as he watched Kirby draw me into an empty classroom.

Kirby and I found the darkest corner of the room, where nobody could see us. "I missed you," she whispered, pulling me close to her.

"I missed you, too."

"Do you have to work tonight?"

"Yeah."

"Too bad." But we made the most of the ten minutes we had left of lunch.

chapter 22

On the surface, the trouble that spring started with Mr. Barent, but I knew Michael was behind it.

Mr. Barent was the advisor for the student literary magazine, *Quill*. It came out twice a year, in winter and spring. I read some of it when I was a freshman, but it was full of stories about Black Mountain parties, and poems by Black Mountain kids about how miserable they were. After that, I never read it except when Julia showed me her poems in it. She was on the staff. Michael was, too.

The first issue after Julia's death—the December issue—had had a photograph of Julia and an article about her, written by the editor. That seemed to wrap up Julia's link with *Quill*. But somehow, that spring, Mr. Barent discovered a file of Julia's work in the *Quill* cabinet, and he decided to publish it in a special section of the spring issue.

I figured that Michael either gave Barent the file or left it where he knew Barent would discover it. I was pretty sure Julia hadn't left these poems sitting around in the *Quill* file cabinet; I thought Michael must've brought them from home. Because they were all poems she'd written to me.

I knew they were for me because she'd shown me some of them, and she'd copied others into the notebook. Lots of them described things we'd done together. Of course, I didn't see this collection—I didn't even know about it—until *Quill* came out at the end of April. It had an introduction written by Michael about how his sister had written these poems, and she'd died a few months ago, and her family wanted to share her art with the world. And by the way, the world might also like to know that she'd written these poems for her boyfriend, Austin. To top it off, there was a photo of Austin and a sickening paragraph written by him that ended, "I love you, Julia baby. Peace forever."

I wanted to puke when I saw this thing. Literally: I felt the sourness creeping up the back of my throat. I saw the magazine in study hall. I'd picked up a copy after hearing people talk about it, but I didn't believe it until I saw it.

The Black Mountain kids thought it was "so beautiful," and some of the girls sighed for poor Austin, who must be having such a hard time. I read Austin's paragraph again, wondering if he actually believed she'd been writing to him. After all, she described things he'd never done with her. One of the poems even referred to my brown hair, and Austin was blond. Didn't Austin find that strange? Didn't Barent? Didn't everyone? Maybe they just saw what they wanted to see.

I couldn't stop reading Austin's stupid paragraph. I was sick of him. Julia's notebook had been full of him; the school halls were full of him. He'd had her 90 percent of the time. Did he have to take my 10 percent, too? He might as well cross out my initials in her notebook, and replace them with his.

I flipped through the pages of *Quill* again, the pages full of scenes from my life that had now become scenes from Austin's life. In the last poem, Julia called the river water liquid ebony. She wrote about us dissolving in it, melting into water where a patch of moon floated. Austin hadn't been there but I had, and now he was swallowing every bit of her left in the world. With Michael's help.

As much as it bothered me, I shouldn't have chosen Kirby to complain to. Any idiot would've known that. All I can say is that anger must've drained the blood away from my brain. I muttered about *Quill* to Kirby at lunch. Everyone else at our table was talking about some party the weekend before, paying no attention to us. So I kept bitching.

"I don't know why they didn't notice Austin is blond," Kirby said. "Give it a rest, Colt."

"And all those lines about the Willis River. Austin never swam in the Willis River in his life."

"So what? What does it matter?"

"Of course, he has so many drunken blackouts, maybe he believes he did swim in the river."

"Shut *up!*" she said. Then everyone at our table looked at us. Everyone at the next table, too.

"I don't want to hear any more about Julia Vernon!" She got up and started walking away from our table.

"Kirby, wait," I said.

She spun around. "No. I'm sick of this shit. So Julia screwed around with you—that's all it was to her! But you—you're still in love with a dead girl. You can have her! I'm not taking this shit anymore."

She stormed away. Everyone at our table stared at me. Behind us was a table of Black Mountain kids, and they stared, too. Four tables full of people were close enough to hear what Kirby had said. I figured it would take maybe an hour and a half for the story to get around the whole school.

"You screwed around with Julia Vernon?" Paul said.

"No shit, Colt?" Nick laughed. "So how was she?"

"Yeah, was she any good?"

"Wait'll Chadwick hears this."

"Oh, you know Colt," Fred drawled. "He can't keep his hands off other people's girls."

I didn't say anything. I didn't know where to look. Then I noticed Syd. She wasn't snickering with everyone else. Her eyes had widened at the news, and I could see the questions in her face, but she wouldn't ask me anything now, here. I kept my eyes on hers until I was able to get up and walk away.

I saw Michael in the hall just before last period. He cringed when he saw me—Michael, who'd kept a stone face through his sister's funeral. I stared at him while the ripple of gossip that had followed me all afternoon rose to a rumble. He rubbed his lips together.

"Was it worth it?" I asked, low so nobody else could hear.

"Jesus, Morrissey. I didn't mean for it to go down like this." At least he didn't try to pretend he had nothing to do with *Quill*. He glanced at the kids who hovered nearby, chewing over the news. "I never thought Kirby would have it out with you in the middle of the cafeteria. I didn't plan for the whole school to know about Julia."

"So much for plans," I said.

That was a Friday. As soon as I got home from school, I called Barney's and said I couldn't work that weekend. I left a note for my parents and packed a bag. Before I left, I thought about calling Kirby, but I called Syd instead.

"Does everybody know?" I asked, roaming around my bedroom with the phone at my ear, the way I had the night Syd told me about the accident.

"Just about. Some of the Black Mountain kids say it's a lie, but I think everyone knows it's true. When you know what to look for, it's right there in the poems. Plus, Michael Vernon isn't denying it."

"What is he saying?"

"Nothing. He won't say anything. That makes people think it must be true."

He wouldn't deny it because I had the notebook. Evidence. Michael had no way of knowing I would never show that book to anyone else. I didn't care what they thought of me, what they wanted me to prove.

Syd went on, "So, last fall, when you told me you were in love with somebody else, you meant Julia, right?"

"Yes."

"I didn't think you even knew her."

"That was the whole idea. Nobody thought we knew each other."

"You sure know how to keep a secret. How did it happen, anyway?"

I stopped pacing and sat on my bed. "We ran into each other one night, down by the river. And then we started meeting there every week or so."

She was quiet for a minute. "You could've told me. I wouldn't have said anything."

"I know."

"Why didn't you?"

"I just—didn't want to tell anyone." How could I explain it? Yes, I could've trusted Syd; I knew her inside out. That was the trouble, that we knew everything about each other. Her feet were planted in the same muddy river soil as mine. With Syd I had nowhere to hide, no chance to be anything but a guy from the flats. And I loved the flats, but sometimes I wanted more than that.

Not that I wanted to be part of Black Mountain either. What would I do with country clubs and servants? I wanted an imaginary place, full of black water and heat and the feel of Julia's skin. Without someone like Syd to anchor me to reality, I could pretend that place existed. I could even believe I belonged there with Julia. Apparently there was no end to the ways I could fool myself.

"It's not like this never happened before," Syd said. "I mean, someone from Black Mountain going out with someone from the flats. Remember Tristan Allen and Jessica Vitale? And Tim Granger and Emily Cavendish?"

"Yeah."

"They didn't try to keep it a secret, though."

"I know."

"Well," Syd said. "It's none of my business, but you could've told me."

I checked the clock: almost time for me to leave. "Do you think Kirby's going to forgive me?"

"For what, lying?"

"I didn't lie to her. She's known about Julia for a while."

"Then what else is there?"

I couldn't explain it. I didn't know anymore if Kirby was wrong to be jealous of Julia, or if she was right that I was still hanging on to the past.

"Colt," Syd said, "even after everything that's happened this year . . . I'm still your friend."

"Thanks," I said. "I could use one."

chapter 23

I took a bus to Tom's school. Actually it was three buses,
two transfers. I got there around ten o'clock Friday night and found
his dorm. People ran up and down the hall, squirting shaving cream
at one another. Through open doors I could see kids studying, watching TV, hanging up wet laundry, and tearing into a pizza. My brother's door was closed. I knocked, wondering what I was going to do if
he wasn't there. It looked like I could crash on one of the couches in
the hall if I had to.

"Yeah," someone, not Tom, yelled from inside.

"It's Colt. I'm looking for Tom Morrissey."

"Colt who?"

"It's my brother!" Tom yelped. The next second he was there in the
doorway facing me, a big grin on his face. "How did you get here?"

"Bus."

"I'll be damned." He led me into the room. His roommate lay on the floor, watching TV and eating microwave popcorn out of a bag. "Hey, Doug, this is Colt."

"Hi, Colt," Doug said, still staring at the TV.

"I can't believe you're here," Tom said. "How long are you going to stay?"

"All weekend, if I can."

"Great! Did you bring your sleeping bag?"

I showed it to him.

"Well, the floor's pretty hard. I'll see if I can dig up an air mattress." He sat on his bed and grinned at me. "Unbelievable! Colten has come to visit." None of our family had come to see him before, even though he'd asked us to. Mom worked too much, and Dad couldn't be bothered, even before Tom's big Thanksgiving announcement. No wonder he was so happy to see me.

We watched TV with Doug for a while, had a pizza, and walked over to another dorm to get an air mattress from a friend of his. While we were walking back across the yard between the buildings, Tom said, "I get the feeling you didn't come up here just for the fun of it."

"Actually, there is something I want to talk to you about."

"Let's sit here awhile then. Doug will still be in his TV trance." He set the crumpled mattress next to a bench and sat down. "Anything wrong back home? Are Mom and Dad okay?"

"They're fine." I sat down, too. "It's me."

"You?"

"Yeah."

"So what is it? You're flunking out of school? You lost your driver's license and you're scared to tell Mom? Or—wait—you got a girl pregnant?"

"God, no. What made you think of all that?"

"You're giving me this lead-in like you're in big trouble, so—"

"No, it's nothing like that. It's—do you remember Julia Vernon?"

"The girl who got killed on Black Mountain last year?"

"Yeah."

"What about her?"

I told him the whole story. About Julia, and the river, and the notebook. About Michael, and Kirby, and the poems in *Quill*. He listened. Even when I was done, he didn't talk. Which for Tom was some kind of miracle, because he *always* had something to say.

"Well?" I asked him. "What do you think?"

"That's quite a story." He ran a hand through his hair. "Are you okay? I can't imagine. . . . If something happened to Derek, I'd lose my mind."

"But it wasn't like she was my girlfriend. She was Austin's."

He chuckled and shook his head. "You spent so much time lying and covering up while she was alive that you don't know when to stop."

"Well, she *wasn't* my girlfriend."

"Who cares about labels? You saw her for a year. Why pretend it didn't affect you?"

"Tom—"

"Like I told you on Thanksgiving, pretending is a lousy way to get through life."

There he went again, with the wise-older-brother routine. "So right after you announced your sexual orientation at the dinner table, I was supposed to jump in with, 'Oh, by the way, I've been screwing around with this girl from Black Mountain, at least I was until she went flying through a windshield, but nobody knows about it because she was too ashamed to tell anyone—'"

"I don't think she was ashamed of you," Tom said. "She was ashamed of herself."

"What for?"

"Lying to Austin. Cheating on him. And never being able to choose between the two of you."

I thought about that. A couple of girls walked past our bench. People sat all over the yard, some of them drinking and smoking. You could smell the beer, see the cigarettes like sparks in the darkness. Tom went on. "And your girlfriend, Kirby, she's right. You're not over this. You're still hanging on to Julia."

"What am I supposed to do? I thought it would end when I finished the notebook. Then I thought it would end when I got that letter from Pam. I thought it was over when I started seeing Kirby. Now I wonder if it's ever going to be over. When is Julia going to get out of my head?"

"I guess that's up to you," Tom said. "Not to sound like a cheesy TV psychologist here, but—"

"Screw that. *She's* the one who won't leave *me* alone. She always knew how to get to me. The last time I saw her—"

Tom waited. When I didn't finish, he said, "What about it?"

I didn't answer. I never liked to think about that night.

"Colt?"

I sucked in my breath. "She died on a Monday, Labor Day. The last time I saw her was the Friday before."

"At the bridge?"

"Yeah, of course." I swallowed.

"So what happened?"

We had sex in her car, as usual. Then she wanted to go wading in the river. All I wanted to do was lie in the backseat and relax, but she dragged me out of the car and into the water. I rolled up my pants. She was wearing shorts.

"School starts Wednesday," she said.

"Yeah."

"I'll be a senior!" She bent low enough to get her hands in the water, and splashed me. "I'll still talk to you, though, even though you're only a junior."

She meant that to be funny, I knew, but it rubbed me the wrong way. "Hell, you don't talk to me as it is; why should you start now?"

"I don't talk to you? What do you think we're doing now?"

"You know what I mean."

She stood up straight and scowled, her hands dripping. "Oh, don't pull this bullshit. You like things exactly the way they are."

"You mean *you* like things the way they are."

She shook water off her hands. Some of the drops hit me. "So what are you saying? You want me to bring you home to meet Mom and Stepdad? You want to come to the country club tomorrow, and go to Adam's party Monday? Is that what you want?" When I didn't say anything, she said, "See, I can call your bluff every time."

"You always say I'd have to turn into Austin. But why should I, since you never stop bitching about him?" Then I said something I'd never said before. "Maybe you should think about coming down to the flats instead."

She stared at me. After a minute, she said, "Don't spoil it, okay? Let's keep things the way they are."

"Fine." I didn't know why I'd started this stupid argument in the first place. I paced circles through the water.

She watched me. I could tell, I could feel her eyes, though I wouldn't look at her. "Colt. Did you tell your friends about us?"

"What? No."

"Come on, did you tell them?"

I glanced over at her. She was frowning. It was the only time I'd ever seen her look the slightest bit afraid. At first I thought it was funny, that such a small thing could scare her, but then it started to piss me off. Would it be so horrible if people did find out about us? Would it kill her to be seen with me? I said, "I told you, no. Why are you even asking?"

"I thought maybe you bragged about us and your friends didn't believe you. Maybe that's why you want to go public all of a sudden."

"Didn't we just agree to forget this whole thing?"

"Okay." She watched me walk around in the river. "I don't know what you want," she said. "Sometimes you act like you love me, and sometimes you act like you couldn't care less."

I turned my back on her. I wasn't in the mood to give her anything right then, to joke with her, to play our usual game. "Then I guess you'll always have to wonder," I said over my shoulder.

She shoved me, hard, in the back, so hard I took two steps forward. I turned on her and grabbed her arms.

"Who the hell do you think you are?" she said. "Don't you *ever* act like you're hot shit just because I let you fuck me."

"What's that supposed to mean?"

"What do you think it means? You're trash and you know it." Her arms trembled. She tried to wrench them free. "Go ahead, tell your friends, tell the whole world. You think they'd believe I touched you?"

My blood burned, sent scorching waves through every part of me. It wasn't just the worst thing she'd ever said to me . . . it was the worst thing anyone had ever said to me. Not because of the words. Anyone from Black Mountain could've called me trash, and it would've bounced off me. What got me was the way she said it, the venom and the total confidence in her voice. The way she made me believe it, because *she* was saying it, Julia, the girl who knew me better and deeper than anyone. She sliced right into me, fed every doubt I'd ever had about myself.

I pushed her away and walked out of the river. She ran after me.

"Colt, I'm sorry."

I kept walking, back toward the car, her shiny perfect car. How did she keep it so shiny?

"I was pissed," she said. "I didn't mean it."

No, she didn't mean it. It was always a game to her. She baited me, and usually I played along. But the whole routine, Rich Girl/Poor Guy, had finally bottomed out. This time she'd hacked deep enough to crack bone.

I stared at that car for another minute. Then I picked up a rock and dragged it down the passenger side. The noise made my teeth ache, but I didn't care. She didn't stop me, either, just stood there with her mouth open while I scratched that gorgeous finish on her gorgeous car. When I got to the rear bumper, I tossed the rock away.

"Colt," she said, as if she needed to say my name to make sure it was still me. As if she didn't recognize the guy who'd just mutilated her car.

We stood there looking at each other. I waited for her to pull Black Mountain rank on me, to tell me she'd call the cops, sue me for the paint job. Instead she took two steps toward me and threw her arms around me. She smelled of perfume and the river, wet hair and sex. She kissed my ear, my neck.

Then I was kissing her, too. She clawed at my clothes and my skin—later I found a few drops of blood on my shirt. And then we were in the backseat again, pushing into each other so hard I thought we'd roll the car over.

When we were done, when we could breathe again, she said, "I'm going to break up with Austin this weekend. I mean it."

I didn't believe her, but she'd wrung me out and I let it pass. "What are you going to tell people about the car?"

"That I scraped against a post, parking."

That's why she didn't take her own car to Adam Hancock's party: hers was in the shop, being painted. She was free to get as drunk as she wanted because she didn't have to drive. That's why Austin drove her to the party and Pam drove her home.

❧ ❧ ❧

"Holy shit," Tom said, when I'd finished.

"Yeah," I said, suddenly tired enough to sleep right there on that bench.

He tilted his head back and looked up at the stars. "It's funny. I lived right down the hall from you last year, and I never knew this was going on."

"That was the point. Nobody was supposed to know."

"Yeah, I can see you got off on the secrecy. So, how'd that work out for you, Colt?"

I started to laugh. "Great. Can't you tell?"

I guess he knew I couldn't talk about it anymore, because he scooped up the mattress. "We'd better get this thing back to the dorm and start blowing it up. I hope it doesn't take all night."

chapter 24

I stayed with Tom all weekend. On Saturday he had to work in the library. I read some of his books, watched TV with his roommate, and walked around the campus for a while. I met him and his boyfriend Derek at a Mexican restaurant for dinner.

Derek shook my hand as if we were a couple of businessmen, then reeled off an original comedy routine all through dinner, complete with celebrity impersonations. Before I met him, I never would've believed that anyone could outtalk my brother. Maybe that was why they'd gotten together.

When Tom went to the bathroom, Derek wound down. "Tom thinks I'm trying too hard, I can tell," he said. "Sorry if I seem a little manic, but you're the first person in his family that I've met. He says your father won't even talk to him, so I don't have too many shots at this."

It struck me as funny that Derek had been trying to impress me.

"Relax," I said. "If you can put up with my brother, you don't have to worry about me."

After dinner, we stopped by a party. It still surprised me for some reason—I guess because it was so new to me—when Tom put his hand on Derek's shoulder or his arm around Derek's waist, but I was getting used to it.

I didn't drink much at the party. I didn't need to. Since I'd told Tom about my last night with Julia, I'd been feeling half high already. I hadn't realized I'd been lugging that night around with me, hadn't felt its weight until I finally let it go. So now I just drank one beer and watched my brother show off his ability to dance on tables without tipping them over, and his skill at making up song parodies on the spot. What with Derek's impersonations, they had a hell of a routine worked out.

I let myself stop thinking about Julia and Kirby and Austin, let myself stop wondering what I was going to do next about that whole mess. I didn't flirt with the girls at the party or try to make them think I was a college student. I didn't try to be anything. I was just there.

I took the bus back on Sunday afternoon. Dad was up, and sober for a change, when I got home. "So you went to see Tommy," he said when I walked in the door.

"Yeah."

"How—how is he?"

"Good."

He cleared his throat. "Did he say when he's coming home?"

Tom had told me he was thinking of staying up at college all summer, working and taking classes. But all I said to my father was, "Why don't you ask him?"

I left the room and took a shower, but I know he called Tom that night.

All day on Monday, kids told me Austin was after me. "He knows where to find me," I said. I think they wanted me to go charging up Black Mountain and tackle him first, but why should I?

I did wonder what I was going to say when he finally confronted me. I had never known if he realized that Julia cheated on him. Even if he'd never suspected me, couldn't he tell there was *somebody*? Didn't he ever notice she kept part of herself back?

Kirby came into the restaurant that night, just before my shift ended. I hadn't seen her since she'd screamed at me in the cafeteria on Friday, and my stomach bucked when I saw her now. I couldn't tell anything from her face.

"You're off soon, aren't you?" she asked.

I checked the clock. "Five minutes."

"I want to talk to you."

"All right." I wiped off my last tables of the night and punched out. We walked to her spot in the parking lot. Before she could say whatever she'd come to say, I told her, "I'm sorry."

"I know you are. But—"

"I don't want to lose you."

She leaned against her mother's car, crossed her arms, and stared at me. "Let me ask you something," she said.

"Okay."

"I called Pam this weekend. She said you told her you felt guilty about Julia. Is that why you're so obsessed? Is that why everything always comes back to Julia?"

I didn't answer.

"Get over yourself," she said. "You weren't even there that night."

I could never explain it to her. I could never tell her what I'd done to Julia's car and why. I did know that even though I'd played my part by scratching the car, I hadn't made Pam skid out on Black Mountain Road. But my guilt was a lot bigger than that. Sometimes I thought the accident was punishment for our having been together at all.

"She wormed right into your brain, didn't she?" Kirby said. "She didn't deserve you." When I didn't say anything, she went on, "Look, I know it makes me sound like the world's biggest bitch to bring it up now, when she's dead. You're probably tired of hearing it."

"I know you never got along with her."

"She was a snob. She once said that Syd should watch out or she'd end up barefoot and pregnant at seventeen, because that's what happened to girls from the flats."

Julia had a horror of getting pregnant before she was ready. As much as we flung ourselves into sex, as much as we risked by being together, we never risked that. My old girlfriend Jackie had once said she'd let me try sex without a condom, "just for a minute, to see what it's like," and God did I want to, but I knew it was a stupid idea so we didn't. Julia would've cut off her own head rather than make me an offer like that. "You don't know what it's like, to worry about something taking over your body, your whole life," she said. And it was probably good she felt that way, because with her I might've been tempted to take stupid risks.

"She looked down on people," Kirby went on. "Julia thought everyone should fall down and worship her. And it kills me to think you fell for that. I mean—did you think you weren't good enough for her?"

"It wasn't like that."

She stared at me, as if waiting for me to go on. I recognized Julia in what Kirby said, the self-confidence that sometimes came off as arrogance. That was the part of Julia I liked the least. But Kirby didn't know the rest. She didn't know the Julia who could laugh at herself, who called me when I had the flu, who liked getting her feet muddy in the river. It would take hours to tell Kirby those things, and even then she might not believe me, because I could never describe all the layers of Julia.

She sighed. "You're so caught up in her. I don't know why you even tried with me."

"I love you."

"You only say that when it's forced out of you."

"It's not easy for me to say . . . but that doesn't mean I don't mean it."

"I know. I love you, too. But Julia keeps getting in the way." She pulled out her car keys. "You need some time to get over this."

"Time away from you, you mean."

"Yes."

We stood there for another minute. She examined her keys as if she'd forgotten what they were for.

I took one step toward her, but she shook her head. So I walked
away, and we got in our cars. She went back to the base of Black
Mountain, while I went home to the flats.

The phone rang sometime after I'd gone to bed. I was the only one
who ever answered it at night, since my mother slept with earplugs,
and my father was usually passed out. Before I put it to my ear, I woke
up enough to think maybe it was Kirby, calling to say she'd changed
her mind.

It wasn't Kirby. It was some guy yelling, but I couldn't understand
what he was saying. He slurred too much. I figured it was one of my
father's drinking buddies. I was about to hang up when I caught the
name "Julia."

"What?" I said.

"You better stop telling your fucking lies about Julia."

I sat up in the dark. "Chadwick?"

"You prick. You think she woulda touched you?"

I took a breath. I'm not sure what I was going to say, but I never
said it, because he started bawling.

When Julia died, I'd watched Austin for signs that he'd taken it
in the gut the way I had. I hadn't seen any at the funeral, where he'd
been his usual polished self, practically posing next to the casket as
if he were an actor in a movie about a funeral. At school he'd looked
solemn, the way people expected him to look, but I couldn't see anything raw in him. But then, who was I to talk? I hadn't gone around
with her death all over my face; I hadn't flung myself into the grave
with her.

I sat there listening, not knowing what to do. I couldn't believe Austin Chadwick was crying in my ear. Maybe I was dreaming.

"Jesus," he sobbed, "why she do it?"

"What?"

"You." He sniffed, then coughed. "She musta been mad at me."

"Austin—"

He inhaled, so loud I could hear it on my end of the phone. "You think she loved you?" Now he was yelling again. "She didn't love you. *She didn't love you.*" And he hung up.

For the rest of the school year, Austin let his eyes skim over me like I wasn't there. I don't think he even remembered that he'd called me. He graduated that spring.

Plenty of Black Mountain kids accused me of outright lying about Julia. Some of the others said she'd been slumming. I'd always thought it meant more than that to her—I was almost positive it was more than that—but I'd never lost that last little piece of doubt.

I called Kirby at the beginning of June, just before finals, but she said, "I'm not ready to talk to you, Colt." She sounded like she might not ever be ready. I realized then we were never going to get back what we'd had. So that was one more thing I would just have to live with.

chapter 25

On the last day of school, I packed Julia's notebook in a box, along with my junior-high diploma, and some other things I didn't need to keep in my room anymore. I stuck the box in the attic, next to the boxes Tom had stowed up there when he went away to college.

I walked down to the bridge. I had always thought of this spot as belonging to Julia and me, although we hadn't always had it to ourselves. A couple of times, I'd found kids partying here and gone home without seeing her.

Once, we were in her backseat when a car pulled up. She had me get on the floor with a coat over me while she buttoned up and looked out the windows. "Some kids I don't recognize," she reported. "Just to be on the safe side, I'll drive us out of here." Sitting there on the gritty floor, muffled by the coat, I felt as low as I'd ever felt with her, like the garbage that had to be swept under the rug when company came. I was about an inch away from ending the whole thing, but she pulled into the lot of an abandoned gas station to let me up. She hissed, "We almost got caught," her eyes bright and her fingers already reaching for me, and I dove into her again like I'd never dreamed of leaving.

All year I'd been walking this riverbank with her voice and the lines of her notebook in my head, living those highs and lows again, trying to keep her. But we'd had only so many nights together, and the notebook had only so many pages, and that world was never going to get any bigger. The truth was that I couldn't have kept her even if she'd lived. At the end, we'd both been pushing at the walls of our secret world, pushing at each other. We'd given each other everything we could. It wasn't enough for either of us anymore; we'd outgrown her backseat.

I walked down to the river's edge and squatted, my boots sinking in the silty muck. I dipped my hands and forearms in the water, splashed it up over my head. The Willis River was always muddy, with a strange moldy smell to it, but on this day it felt clean.

▪ *acknowledgments* ▪

I owe thanks to all the people who gave me feedback, support, and encouragement while I worked on this book, and to those who helped shape it and bring it to the bookshelves. I couldn't have done this without the amazing Nathan Bransford and the wonderful people at Viking, including Sam Kim, Abigail Powers, and especially Catherine Frank.

I am grateful for the friendship and support of Teresa Bonaddio, Kelly Fineman, and Colleen Rowan Kosinski. Thanks also to Jessica Dimuzio (VMD) and the Milestones Critique Circle of Chestnut Hill; and the online communities of Debut2009 and 10_ers. It's been my privilege to interact with the Classes of 2k9 and 2k10.

Special thanks and love to my family: my parents, James and Cheryl; my sister Bonnie; my grandmothers, Dorothy and Jane; my grandfathers, Bradford and Clarence; my stepson Will; and most of all, John, the best husband in the world.